Voltaire,

born François-Marie Arouet in Paris in 1694, was educated by Jesuits at the Collège le Grand. Increasingly dissatisfied with much of French society, he expressed his displeasure by satirizing many rich and powerful Frenchmen, despite his own love of the pomp that accompanied power and money. For mocking the regent, he was imprisoned in the Bastille in 1717, where he wrote his first tragedy, *Oedipe* (1718). He was released after two years. Sent there again in 1726, he was soon paroled on condition that he leave France.

Voltaire spent the next three years exiled in England, where he met Pope, Congreve and Swift, and developed a great admiration for the English. He continued to study French society from abroad and to condemn its corruption. His observations on France and England were published after his return to France in 1729. *Letters Concerning the English Nation* (1734) caused such an uproar for its recommendation of the English system over the French that he was forced to flee Paris.

After his escape, Voltaire settled in Lorraine with a young woman of learning, Madame du Châtelet, who encouraged Voltaire's literary efforts. While in her company, he began work on one of his most noted works, *Le Siècle de Louis XIV* (1751), several historical tragedies and a translation of Newton's *Principia*.

After Madame du Châtelet's death in 1749, Voltaire moved to Berlin, where he served as chamberlain to Frederick II of Prussia; again, he was forced to flee after a falling out with the king. In 1752, Voltaire's major philosophical work, the massive *Encyclopédie*, was published. In 1753, he moved to a French estate outside Geneva, at Ferney, and settled there with his niece. It was here that Voltaire completed his most acrid, satirical and famous work, *Candide* (1759). After many years he returned triumphantly to Paris in 1778 and was awarded a laurel wreath at the theater where his hugely successful play *Irene* was being performed. Voltaire never left Paris again: he died there on May 30, 1778.

Bantam Classics
Ask your bookseller for these other World Classics

GREEK DRAMA, edited by Moses Hadas

THE COMPLETE PLAYS OF SOPHOCLES

TEN PLAYS, Euripides

THE COMPLETE PLAYS OF ARISTOPHANES

PLAUTUS: THREE COMEDIES (translated by Erich Segal)

THE AENEID, Virgil (translated by Allen Mandelbaum)

INFERNO, Dante (translated by Allen Mandelbaum)
PURGATORIO, Dante (translated by Allen Mandelbaum)

THE PRINCE, Machiavelli

CANDIDE, Voltaire

FAUST, Johann Wolfgang von Goethe

THE COUNT OF MONTE CRISTO, Alexandre Dumas
THE THREE MUSKETEERS, Alexandre Dumas

THE HUNCHBACK OF NOTRE DAME, Victor Hugo

MADAME BOVARY, Gustave Flaubert

FATHERS AND SONS, Ivan Turgenev

ANNA KARENINA, Leo Tolstoy
THE DEATH OF IVAN ILYICH, Leo Tolstoy

THE BROTHERS KARAMAZOV, Fyodor Dostoevsky
CRIME AND PUNISHMENT, Fyodor Dostoevsky
THE IDIOT, Fyodor Dostoevsky
NOTES FROM UNDERGROUND, Fyodor Dostoevsky

CYRANO DE BERGERAC, Edmond Rostand

20,000 LEAGUES UNDER THE SEA, Jules Verne
AROUND THE WORLD IN EIGHTY DAYS, Jules Verne

FOUR GREAT PLAYS, Henrik Ibsen

FIVE MAJOR PLAYS, Anton Chekhov

THE METAMORPHOSIS, Franz Kafka

Candide
by Voltaire

Translated by Lowell Bair

With an appreciation by André Maurois
Illustrations by Sheilah Beckett

BANTAM BOOKS

TORONTO · NEW YORK · LONDON · SYDNEY · AUCKLAND

The original edition of 1759 did not appear under Voltaire's name, and he denied being its author. It bore this title: "Candide, or Optimism. Translated from the German of Dr. Ralph." In 1761 an edition appeared in which Voltaire had made a long addition to Chapter XXII (included in the present translation). The title of this edition was: "Candide, or Optimism. Translated from the German of Dr. Ralph. With the additions found in the Doctor's pocket when he died at Minden, in the Year of Grace 1759."

CANDIDE
A Bantam Book / December 1959

An appreciation extracted from Voltaire by André Maurois
Copyright 1932, D. Appleton & Company. Reprinted by
permission of the publishers, Appleton-Century-Crofts, Inc.

Bantam Classic edition / March 1981
2nd printing .... August 1981   4th printing ...... February 1983
3rd printing .... April 1982   5th printing ..... September 1983
6th printing ... May 1984

Cover painting, "Playground in the Garden" (detail), by Jean-Demosthene Dugourc. Courtesy of the Metropolitan Museum of Art.

Library of Congress Catalog Card Number: 59-11563

ISBN 0-553-21166-8

Published simultaneously in the United States and Canada

Bantam Books are published by Bantam Books, Inc. Its trademark, consisting of the words "Bantam Books" and the portrayal of a rooster, is Registered in U.S. Patent and Trademark Office and in other countries. Marca Registrada. Bantam Books, Inc., 666 Fifth Avenue, New York, New York 10103.

PRINTED IN THE UNITED STATES OF AMERICA

O   15 14 13 12 11 10 9

Contents

An Appreciation by André Maurois.   1

I   How Candide was brought up in a beautiful castle, and how he was driven from it.   17

II   What happened to Candide among the Bulgars.   19

III   How Candide escaped from the Bulgars, and what happened to him.   22

IV   How Candide met his former philosophy teacher, Dr. Pangloss, and what ensued.   25

V   Storm, shipwreck and earthquake, and what happened to Dr. Pangloss, Candide and James the Anabaptist.   28

VI   How a fine auto-da-fé was performed to prevent earthquakes, and how Candide was flogged.   31

VII   How an old woman took care of Candide, and how he found the object of his love.   32

VIII   Cunegonde's story.   34

IX   What happened to Cunegonde, Candide, the Grand Inquisitor and the Jew.   37

X   How Candide, Cunegonde and the old woman arrived at Cadiz in great distress, and how they set sail from there.   40

XI   The old woman's story.   42

XII	Further misfortunes of the old woman.	46
XIII	How Candide was forced to leave the fair Cunegonde and the old woman.	49
XIV	How Candide and Cacambo were received by the Jesuits of Paraguay.	52
XV	How Candide killed the brother of his beloved Cunegonde.	55
XVI	What happened to the two travelers with two girls, two monkeys, and the savages known as the Oreillons.	57
XVII	How Candide and his valet came to the land of Eldorado.	62
XVIII	What they saw in the land of Eldorado.	66
XIX	What happened to them at Surinam, and how Candide became acquainted with Martin.	72
XX	What happened to Candide and Martin at sea.	77
XXI	How Candide and Martin reasoned with each other as they approached the coast of France.	79
XXII	What happened to Candide and Martin in France.	81
XXIII	How Candide and Martin reached the coast of England, and what they saw there.	92
XXIV	Paquette and Brother Giroflée.	93
XXV	A visit to Signor Pococurante, Venetian nobleman.	99
XXVI	How Candide and Martin had supper with six foreigners, and who they were.	104
XXVII	Candide's voyage to Constantinople.	107
XXVIII	What happened to Candide, Cunegonde, Pangloss, Martin, etc.	111
XXIX	How Candide found Cunegonde and the old woman again.	115
XXX	Conclusion.	116
	Notes.	121

The Sage of Ferney

AN APPRECIATION
by André Maurois

In the eyes of posterity, nearly every great man is stabilized at one age of life. The Byron of legend is the handsome youth of 1812, not the full-grown man, prematurely ageing, with thinning hair, whom Lady Blessington knew. Tolstoy is the shaggy old peasant with a broad girdle circling his rustic blouse. The Voltaire of legend is the thin, mischievous old man of Ferney, as Houdon carved him, sneering, his skeleton form bent under its white marble dressing-gown, but bent as a spring is bent, ready to leap. For twenty years Voltaire, at Ferney, was a dying man: he had been one all his life. "But in his health, about which he was for ever complaining, he had a valuable prop which he used to wonderful advantage: for Voltaire's constitution was robust enough to withstand the most extreme mental activity, yet frail enough to make any other excess difficult to sustain."

His Ferney retreat was populous. Voltaire said that sages retire into solitude and become sapless with ennui. At Ferney he knew neither ennui nor solitude. His circle there included, first, his two nieces: Mme. Denis was "a round, plump little woman of about fifty, a rather impossible creature, plain and good-

1

natured, an unintentional and harmless liar; devoid of wit and with no semblance of having any; shouting, deciding things, talking politics, versifying, talking reason, talking nonsense; in everything quite unpretentious and certainly shocking nobody." Voltaire had purchased Ferney in her name, conditionally on her signing a private reservation for his usufruct; but on completion of the purchase she refused to sign this document, not to expel her uncle, but to hold him in her power, a circumstance which was the root of a great quarrel. Mme. de Fontaine, the other niece, was more appealing and manageable; she was particularly fond of painting, and filled the house with beautiful nudes after Natoire and Boucher, "to quicken her uncle's ageing blood." He relished these. "One should have some copying done at the Palais Royal," he wrote to her, "of whatever is most beautiful and most immodest there."

The two nieces came and went; the permanent guests were a secretary, the faithful Wagnière, and a Jesuit, Father Adam. It may seem surprising to find a Jesuit in Voltaire's old age, but in his heart of hearts he retained a certain fondness for the Reverend Fathers "who had reared him nicely enough." Father Adam was a great chess player and had a daily game with Voltaire. "This good Father," said the latter, "may not be one of the world's great men, but he understands very well the way this game goes." When the priest was winning Voltaire would overturn the board. "Imagine spending two hours in moving little bits of wood to and fro!" he exclaimed. "One could have written an act of a tragedy in the time." When he himself was winning, he would play the game out.

It was the Father who said his Mass, for one of Voltaire's first acts at Ferney was to build a church there. Over its porch was put the proud inscription: *Deo Erexit Voltaire.* "Two great names," remarked the visitors. Voltaire had also had constructed a tomb for himself, half inside the church and half in the graveyard. "The rascals," he explained, "will say that I'm neither in nor out." He had also built a room for stage performances. "If you meet any of the devout, tell them I've built a church; if you meet pleasant people, tell them I've finished a theatre."

The village of Ferney was transformed under his hands to a thriving little town. He cleared land. He built houses for the workers on the land and let them have homes on very easy terms. "I have left abundance where there was want before. True—only by ruining myself. But a man could not ruin himself in a more decent cause."

To people his town he took advantage of certain persecutions then proceeding in Geneva. He set up workshops to make silk stockings. He established a lace-making industry. Above all, he attracted to his seat excellent watchmakers, and took as much trouble to market the watches of his subjects as to administer an empire. He recommended the Ferney watches to all his friends in Paris: "They make them much better here than at Geneva. . . For eighteen *louis* you will get an excellent repeater here which would cost you forty in Paris. Send your orders and they will be fulfilled. . . You shall have splendid watches and very bad verses, whenever you fancy."

In fine, he had made Ferney into a small paradise, active and cheerful, and all the happier because its religious toleration was perfect: "In my hamlet, where I have made more than a hundred Genevese and their families at home, nobody notices that there are two religions."

Age only augmented his craving for activity and his zest in work: "The further I advance along the path of life," he wrote, "the more do I find work a necessity. In the long run it becomes the greatest of pleasures, and it replaces all one's lost illusions." And again: "Neither my old age nor my illnesses dishearten me. Had I cleared but one field and made but twenty trees to flourish, that would still be an imperishable boon." The philosophy of *Candide* is drawing near.

Legend is not wrong in seeing the Voltaire of Ferney as the true Voltaire. Before Ferney, what was he? A very famous poet and playwright, a much-discussed historian, a popularizer of science: France regarded him as a brilliant writer, not as an intellectual force. It was Ferney that freed him, and so made him great. The battle for freedom of thought which his friends the Encyclopedists had engaged upon, and could not carry on in Paris without danger, was to be directed by him from his retreat. To that struggle he contributed wit and fancy, an infinite variety in forms, a deliberate uniformity in ideas.

For twenty years Ferney discharged over Europe a hail of pamphlets printed under scores of names, forbidden, confiscated, disowned, denied, but hawked, read, admired, and digested by all the thinking heads of that time. Voltaire at Ferney was no longer the "fashionable man"; he was a Benedictine of rationalism. He believed in his apostolic mission: "I have done more in my own time," he said, "than Luther and Calvin." And further: "I am tired of hearing it declared that twelve men sufficed to establish Christianity, and I want to prove to them that it only needs one to destroy it." Nearly all his letters ended with the famous formula: *"Ecrasons l'infâme"*—"We must crush the vile thing"—or, as he wrote it with ingenuous caution, *"Ecr. l'inf."* What was the vile thing? Religion? The Church? To be more exact, it was Superstition. He hounded it down because he had suffered from it, and because he believed that bigotry makes men more unhappy than they need be.

A great part of Voltaire's work at Ferney, then, was destructive. He wanted to show: (a) that it is absurd to suppose that an omnipotent God, creator of Heaven and Earth, had chosen the Jews, a small tribe of Bedouin nomads, as His chosen people; (b) that the chronicle of that race (the Bible) was packed with incredible facts, obscenities, and contradictions (he took the trouble to publish, under the title of *La Bible Expliquée*, a survey of the biblical text with countless notes); (c) that the Gospels, although more moral than the Old Testament, were nevertheless full of the gossipings of illiterate nobodies; and finally (d) that the

4

disputes which set the sects at each other's throats throughout eighteen centuries were foolish and unavailing.

The Voltairean criticism has been itself criticized. It has been said that Voltaire lacks sympathy and proportion, and that in any case his own historical science was often at fault. But we must be fair. Voltaire often made particular effort to be so himself. "It cannot be too often repeated," he said, "that we must not judge these centuries by the measure of our own, nor the Jews by that of Frenchmen or Englishmen." If we are prepared to view the Bible as a collection of legends compiled by barbarian tribes, then he is prepared to admit that it is "as captivating as Homer." If we claim to find therein a divine utterance and super-human thoughts, then he claims the right to quote the prophets, and show their cruel savagery.

What is Voltaire's positive philosophy? It is an agnosticism tempered by a deism. "It is natural to admit the existence of a God as soon as one opens one's eyes. . . The creation betokens the Creator. It is by virtue of an admirable art that all the planets dance round the sun. Animals, vegetables, minerals—everything is ordered with proportion, number, movement. Nobody can doubt that a painted landscape or drawn animals are works of skilled artists. Could copies possibly spring from an intelligence and the originals not?"

Regarding the nature of God he has little to teach us. "Fanatics tell us: God came at such-and-such a time; in a certain small town God preached, and He hardened the hearts of His listeners so that they might have no faith in Him; He spoke to them and they stopped their ears. Now, the whole world should laugh at these fanatics. I shall say as much of all the gods that have been invented. I shall be no more merciful to the monsters of the Indies than to the monsters of Egypt. I shall blame every nation that has abandoned the universal God for all these phantoms of private gods."

What, then, is to be believed? That is rather vague.

5

"The great name of theist is the only one that should be borne; the only book that should be read is the great book of nature. The sole religion is to worship God and to be an honorable man. This pure and ever-lasting religion cannot possibly produce harm." And certainly it would seem difficult for this theism to produce harm; but is it capable of producing much good? It is incomprehensible how so hollow and abstract a belief will maintain the weight of a moral system, and the moral system of Voltaire is not actually based on his theism. It is a purely human morality.

A theist in name, a humanist in fact—that is Voltaire. When he wishes seriously to justify a moral precept, he does so through the idea of society. Moreover, as God is everywhere, morality is in nature itself. "There is something of divinity in a flea." At all times and in all places man has found a single morality in his own heart. Socrates, Jesus, and Confucius have differing metaphysics, but more or less the same moral system. Replying to Pascal—who found it "pleasing" that men such as robbers, who have renounced all the laws of God, should contrive other laws which they scrupulously obey—Voltaire wrote: "That is more useful than pleasing to consider, for it proves that no society can live for a single day without laws. In this, all societies are like games: without rules, they do not exist." Here the historian has seen aright, and with a penetrating phrase has pointed out what modern observers of primitive societies have since described.

Stern judgment has been passed on this Voltairean philosophy. Faguet defined it as "a chaos of clear ideas"; Taine remarked that "he dwarfed great things by dint of bringing them within reach"; and a woman once said: "What I cannot forgive him, is having made me understand so many things which I shall never understand." It is certain that a system imbued with perfect clarity has few chances of being a truthful image of an obscure and mysterious world. But still, it remains probable that this world is in part intelligible, for otherwise there would be neither physics or mechanics.

6

Voltaire himself indicated better than anyone the limitations of clarity, and how much madness and confusion there are in human destinies. Let doubters turn back to the second part of the article on "Ignorance" in the *Philosophical Dictionary:* "I am ignorant of how I was formed and how I was born. Through a quarter of my lifetime I was absolutely ignorant of the reasons for everything I saw and heard and felt, and was merely a parrot prompted by other parrots. . . When I sought to advance along that infinite course, I could neither find one single footpath nor fully discover one single object, and from the upward leap I made to contemplate eternity I fell back into the abyss of my ignorance." Here Voltaire touched hands with Pascal, but only half-way; and this troubled Voltaire is the best Voltaire, for he is the Voltaire of *Candide.*

The author of *Zaïre* and the *Henriade* would doubtless have been prodigiously surprised had he been assured that the only book (or nearly the only book) of his which would continue to be read, and held as a masterpiece of man's wit, would be a short novel written at the age of sixty-five, and bearing the title of *Candide.*

He wrote it to ridicule the optimism of Leibniz. "Everything is for the best in the best of worlds. . . " said the optimists. Voltaire had observed men's lives; he had lived, battled, suffered, and seen suffering. No, emphatically: this world of stakes and scaffolds, battles and disease, was not the best of possible worlds. Some historians—Michelet especially—have attributed the pessimism of *Candide* to particular occurrences: the dreadful earthquake of Lisbon (on which Voltaire wrote a poem), or the Seven Years' War and its victims, or the greed of Mme. Denis. These petty reasons seem useless. Voltaire denied the perfection of the world because, to an intelligent old man, it did not look perfect.

His theme was simple. It was a novel of apprenticeship, that is, the shaping of an adolescent's ideas by rude contact with the universe. Candide learned to know armies and the Jesuits of Paraguay: murder, theft, and rape; France, England, and the Grand Turk. Everywhere his observations showed him that man was rather a wicked animal. Optimist philosophy was personified in Pangloss; pessimism, in Martin, who thinks that man "is born to live either in the convulsions of distress or the lethargy of boredom." But the author accepted neither Martin's pessimism nor Pangloss's optimism at their face values. The last words of the book were: "We must cultivate our garden"; that is to say: the world is mad and cruel; the earth trembles and the sky hurls thunderbolts; kings fight and Churches rend each other. Let us limit our activity and try to do as well as we can the small task that seems to be within our powers.

It is, as René Berthelot remarks, an eminently scientific and bourgeois conclusion. Action is necessary. All is not well, but all things can be bettered. Man "cannot obliterate the cruelty of the universe, but by prudence he can shield certain small confines from that cruelty." What Voltaire sets up against Martin's pessimism and Pangloss's optimism, what he opposes to Christian theology and to the stoic optimism resumed by Leibniz, is Newtonian science, the science that limits itself to nature, that makes us grasp only certain connections, but at least assures us thereby of our power over certain natural phenomena.

No work shows better than *Candide* how fully Voltaire remains a great classic and a man of the eighteenth century, while Rousseau is already a romantic and a man of the nineteenth. Nothing would have been easier than to make *Candide* into a *Childe Harold*. Let Candide take on the semblance of a projection of Voltaire's own personality, let him accuse the Universe of having robbed him of Mlle. Cunegonde, let him conceive of a personal struggle between himself and Destiny—and he would be a romantic hero. But Candide is universal as a character of Molière's is universal; and it was the reading of *Candide* that shaped the second Byron, the anti-romantic, the Byron of *Don Juan*. That is why all romantics are anti-Voltairean, even Michelet, whose political fervor ought to have made him stand aligned with Voltaire; and that is why, on the other hand, all the minds which accept the world and recognize its irony and indifference are Voltairean. It is reported that the eminent journalist, Charles Maurras, re-reads his *Candide* once a year, and as he closes it, says to himself: "The road is clear"—that is to say, that Voltaire sweeps earthly illusions boldly aside, drives away the clouds and all that is interposed between reality and understanding.

One reason for the enduring success of *Candide* is that it represents one of the attitudes of the human mind, and perhaps the bravest. But above all, it is admirable as a work of art. It has been justly observed that the style of *Candide* resembles that of the *Arabian Nights* in Galland's translation. The union of classic French—proving and deducing consequences with such clarity—and the fantastic image of life formed by the fatalist Orient, was bound to produce a novel dissonance. For the poetry of a text is largely produced by the fact that the wild chaos of the universe is therein, at one and the same time, expressed and controlled by a rhythm. In *Candide* both characteristics exist. Over every page stream unforeseeable cascades of facts, and yet the swift movement, the regular recurrence of the optimist themes of Pangloss, the pessimist themes of Martin, the narratives of the old woman and the refrains of Candide, afford the mind that troubled, tragic repose which is only given by great poetry.

Alongside the Galland influence, that of Swift should be noted. Voltaire had read much of Swift, and was fond of him; and from the Dean he had learned how to tell an absurd story in the most natural manner. Of all the classic French texts, *Candide* is certainly the most closely akin to the English humorists. But Swift's rather fierce humor, sometimes too emphatic, is here tempered by the desire to please. In the body of every writer's creation there are things of sheer delight: *Candide* was the best of such in Voltaire's.

During the next twenty years Voltaire worked hard at Ferney, producing there the most important part of his work. It was there that he completed the great labors started at Cirey and at Potsdam: the *Essay on Morals,* the history of *Russia under Peter the Great,* and the *Philosophical Dictionary.* The *Dictionary* is a collection of notes arranged alphabetically, unified only by its underlying doctrine. The idea had been suggested to Voltaire during a supper-party with Frederick the Great; it was bound to attract a man who enjoyed talking of everything and had no love for "composing" in the formal seventeenth-century sense.

There is in existence a history of French clarity; it would be instructive to sketch a history of the French vagary and of uncomposed works, which would bring together Montaigne's *Essays,* the *Characters* of La Bruyère, Voltaire's *Dictionary,* and the *Analecta* of Paul Valéry. The *Essay on Morals* itself is only a kind of encyclopedia with articles ranged in chronological order. The dictionary form suited Voltaire so well that he fell back upon it several times. In 1764 a first volume appeared, which was seized and publicly burnt. Then came the *Questions Touching the Encyclopedia,* and lastly the *Alphabetic Opinion.* After Voltaire's death the whole was merged into the *Philosophical Dictionary* of the Kehl edition, containing anecdotes, theology, science, history, music, verse, and dialogues.

At Ferney, too, Voltaire wrote numerous philosophic tales, and several of these, although falling short of the perfection of *Candide,* are amusing and penetrating. *Jeannot and Colin* should be read, a pleasing and ingenuous satire on the wealthy; *The Man with Forty Crowns,* too, an economic pamphlet rather than a novel; the *History of Jenni,* which has an opening chapter in the best Voltaire vein; and then *The Simpleton,* the *Princess of Babylon, The*

White Bull, and lastly, *White and Black,* which has something of the poetry of *Candide* without its full power.

But the greater part of this mass of work is composed of pamphlets, small books and dialogues, which made Voltaire (along with Addison) the greatest journalist whom men have known. To set forth his ideas and make game of the ideas of his opponents, he created a whole race of puppets: there were the letters of a Hindu victim of the Inquisitors (the *Letters of Amabed*), the theological inquiries of a Spanish licentiate (the *Questions of Zapata*), the advice of the guardian of the Ragusa Capuchins to Brother Pediculoso on his setting forth for the Holy Land—"the first thing you will do, Brother Pediculoso, is to go and see the earthly paradise where God created Adam and Eve, so familiar to the ancient Greeks and early Romans, to the Persians, Egyptians, and Syrians, that none of them ever mentioned it. . . . You need only ask the way of the Capuchins in Jerusalem; you can't get lost." There is the canonization of Saint Cucufin, brother of Ascoli, by Pope Clement XIII, and his miraculous appearance to Monsieur Avelin, citizen of Troyes. There is the sermon of Rabbi Akib, and a rescript of the Emperor of China, and the journey of Brother Garassise, poisoned by the journal of the Jesuits and saved by fragments of the *Encyclopedia,* which dissolve for him in a little white wine.

Wit sometimes fails this polemical literature. The *Canonization of Saint Cucufin* is a clumsy and humorless joke. But the contemporary reader was certain to be delighted by the movement and the intoxicating rhythm of most of these fantasies, their gaiety, their glittering style, and above all by their topical quality. And the contemporary could appreciate more than we can the courage of the polemicist. For all his stature and his strongholds, he was still menaced from time to time. Queen Maria Lecszinska, on her deathbed, asked that his impiousness be punished. "What can I do, madame?" answered the King. "If he were in Paris I should exile him to Ferney." Less reasonable than the sovereign, the Parliament ordered the burning of the *Man with Forty Crowns,* and pilloried a luckless bookseller who had sold a copy. When the case was called, one of the magistrates exclaimed in the criminal court: "Is it only his books we shall burn?" Notwithstanding the proximity of the Swiss frontier, Voltaire was often seized by panic, but he could not resist his demon.

Candide, the tales, and the *Century of Louis XIV* are beyond doubt Voltaire's masterpieces, but in order to understand why and how he exercised so wide an influence over the France of his time, it is necessary to skim his numerous topical writings, ephemeral in subject but not in form, and to imagine what power over opinion was yielded by this journalist of genius, who, tirelessly handling the same themes, was able to astound, excite, and dominate France for over twenty years.

Lives which have made a great stir on earth do not sink at once into the silent sleep of the tomb. The brilliant, dancing *allegretto* of Voltaire's life could not pass abruptly into an *andante maestoso.* For some time longer his royal friends continued to bestir themselves. Frederick II ordered a bust by Houdon. Catherine was anxious to buy his library, asking this in a letter addressed to Mme. Denis, "the niece of a great man who loved me a little."

In France, a Revolution of which he would not have approved (for he was a conservative and monarchist), but for which he had paved the way, treated him as a prophet. In 1791 the Constituent Assembly ordered the transference of Voltaire's ashes to the Pantheon. It was a fine procession, at the head of which went "Belle et Bonne" weeping, in a Greek robe. In 1814 at the time of the Restoration, the sarcophagus was profaned in circumstances which have remained mysterious. Nobody knows what has become of the frail skeleton and "the fleshless bones" which for over eighty years supported with their flimsy framework the noble genius of M. de Voltaire.

Diderot, d'Alembert, and Montesquieu had perhaps played just as great a role in the transformation of eighteenth-century France. But Voltaire and Rousseau have remained, both to Frenchmen and to the world in general, the two symbolic figures of that period. Voltaire stands for its satiric and destructive facet, Rousseau for the popular and sentimental facet. Throughout the nineteenth century battles raged round these two names. In that long warfare between Church and State, which ended (if it did end) at the time of the Dreyfus Affair with the victory of the State, Voltaire was the sacred writer of the Church's adversaries. Voltairean became a regular adjective, defined in one famous dictionary as a man who "has feelings of mocking incredulity regarding Christianity." M. Homais in Flaubert's *Madame Bovary* was a Voltairean: "*Ecrasez l'infâme,*" he kept repeating. Certain critics have treated Voltaire as if he were merely a M. Homais; but others have felt that M. Homais and Voltaire were both necessary, and that Voltaire even did a service to truly religious minds by making an abrupt separation of religion and persecution.

Was his character great? He was complex. He laughed at kings and flattered them. To the Churches he preached forgiveness of insults, and did not show his own enemies mercy. He was generous and miserly, frank and untruthful, cowardly and brave. He had the fear of blows which is natural to human beings, but all his life long he flung himself into affairs where he could receive blows. At Ferney he was like a hare in its form, but a fierce one, a hare which in the jungle of politics sometimes held a lion at bay. He had always great difficulty in resisting the bait of a profitable deal, but still more in abstaining from a dangerous act of beneficence.

Was his intelligence great? He was inquisitive about everything. He knew more history than the mathematicians, and more physics than the historians. He could mold his genius with ease to very diverse disciplines. Such universal minds, it may be thought, are not deeply versed in any subject, and "vulgarization" is sometimes mistaken for "vulgarity"; but that in itself is rather shallow thinking. It is essential that syntheses should be made from time to time, and that inquiring minds should digest the work of the specialists for the benefit of men at large. Failing this, an unbridgeable gulf would appear between the expert and the man-in-the-street, and this would be a great anomaly. Besides, "clarity" is not synonymous with "vulgarity," except perhaps in poetry, and that is why Voltaire is a poet only in his tales, where he laid aside his "clarity."

Had he a great heart? He loathed suffering, for others as for himself, and he helped mankind in the task of avoiding dreadful and useless suffering. A friend once found him reading certain historical topics with tears in his eyes. "Ah!" said Voltaire, "how wretched men have been, and how much to be pitied! And they were wretched only because they were cowards and fools." He was rarely a fool, and never a coward when torture and intolerance had to be fought. "Yes, I say things over and over again," he exclaimed. "That's the privilege of my age, and I'll say them over and over and over again until my fellow-countrymen are cured of their folly." There may be matter for astonishment that he was not ill-disposed toward war, which is one form of torture, and one of the worst; but he lived in a time when wars were waged by professional armies, which was a very intelligent method, and a comparatively harmless one.

Why, among all the eighteenth-century philosophers, does this quite unphilosophical man stand out as the greatest? Perhaps it is because that century, at once bourgeois and gentlemanly, universal and frivolous, scientific and fashionable, European and dominantly French, was most fully reflected in the person of Voltaire, who was in himself all of these things.

Add, that he was extremely French, in the sense that other countries use the term. The rest of this planet has always liked in France the writers, who, like Voltaire or Anatole France, express simple ideas with clarity, wit, and polish. That particular blend is not the whole of France, but it is part of France, and in the best Frenchmen there is always a little of it present. It was in some measure due to Voltaire that French, in the eighteenth century, was the supreme language of Europe, and the glory of that tongue, coruscating in the mirrors of the European Courts, encircled the old man of Ferney with a startling resplendence.

Finally, and above all else, he was marvelously alive; and mankind, dreading boredom even more than anxieties, is grateful to those who make life throb with a swifter, stronger beat. In the downpour of pamphlets, epistles, stories, poems, and letters that was showered on France for so many years from Cirey and Berlin and Ferney, there were trivialities and excellences. But everything was swift and bright, and Frenchmen felt their wits coming alive to the tune of M. de Voltaire's fiddling. A graver music some may prefer; but his must have had charm in plenty, for after more than a century France has not yet wearied of what has been so well called the *prestissimo* of Voltaire.

CHAPTER I

*How Candide was brought up in a beautiful
castle, and how he was driven from it.*

IN the castle of Baron Thunder-ten-tronckh in Westphalia, there once lived a youth endowed by nature
with the gentlest of characters. His soul was revealed
in his face. He combined rather sound judgment with
great simplicity of mind; it was for this reason, I
believe, that he was given the name of Candide. The
old servants of the household suspected that he was
the son of the baron's sister by a good and honorable
gentleman of the vicinity, whom this lady would never
marry because he could prove only seventy-one generations of nobility, the rest of his family tree having
been lost, owing to the ravages of time.

The baron was one of the most powerful lords in
Westphalia, for his castle had a door and windows. Its
hall was even adorned with a tapestry. The dogs in his
stable yards formed a hunting pack when necessary,
his grooms were his huntsmen, and the village curate
was his chaplain. They all called him "My Lord" and
laughed when he told stories.

The baroness, who weighed about three hundred
fifty pounds, thereby winning great esteem, did the
honors of the house with a dignity that made her still
more respectable. Her daughter Cunegonde, aged

seventeen, was rosy-cheeked, fresh, plump and alluring. The baron's son appeared to be worthy of his father in every way. The tutor Pangloss was the oracle of the household, and young Candide listened to his teachings with all the good faith of his age and character.

Pangloss taught metaphysico-theologo-cosmonigology. He proved admirably that in this best of all possible worlds, His Lordship's castle was the most beautiful of castles, and Her Ladyship the best of all possible baronesses.

"It is demonstrated," he said, "that things cannot be otherwise: for, since everything was made for a purpose, everything is necessarily for the best purpose. Note that noses were made to wear spectacles; we therefore have spectacles. Legs were clearly devised to wear breeches, and we have breeches. Stones were created to be hewn and made into castles; His Lordship therefore has a very beautiful castle: the greatest baron in the province must have the finest residence. And since pigs were made to be eaten, we eat pork all year round. Therefore, those who have maintained that all is well have been talking nonsense: they should have maintained that all is for the best."

Candide listened attentively and believed innocently, for he found Lady Cunegonde extremely beautiful, although he was never bold enough to tell her so. He concluded that, after the good fortune of having been born Baron Thunder-ten-tronckh, the second greatest good fortune was to be Lady Cunegonde; the third, to see her every day; and the fourth, to listen to Dr. Pangloss, the greatest philosopher in the province, and therefore in the whole world.

One day as Cunegonde was walking near the castle in the little wood known as "the park," she saw Dr. Pangloss in the bushes, giving a lesson in experimental physics to her mother's chambermaid, a very pretty and docile little brunette. Since Lady Cunegonde was deeply interested in the sciences, she breathlessly observed the repeated experiments that were performed before her eyes. She clearly saw the doctor's sufficient reason, and the operation of cause and effect. She then returned home, agitated and thoughtful, reflecting that she might be young Candide's sufficient reason, and he hers.

On her way back to the castle she met Candide. She blushed, and so did he. She greeted him in a faltering voice, and he spoke to her without knowing what he was saying. The next day, as they were leaving the table after dinner, Cunegonde and Candide found themselves behind a screen. She dropped her handkerchief, he picked it up; she innocently took his hand, and he innocently kissed hers with extraordinary animation, ardor and grace; their lips met, their eyes flashed, their knees trembled, their hands wandered. Baron Thunder-ten-tronckh happened to pass by the screen; seeing this cause and effect, he drove Candide from the castle with vigorous kicks in the backside. Cunegonde fainted. The baroness slapped her as soon as she revived, and consternation reigned in the most beautiful and agreeable of all possible castles.

CHAPTER II

What happened to Candide among the Bulgars.

AFTER being driven from his earthly paradise, Candide walked for a long time without knowing where he was going, weeping, raising his eyes to heaven, looking back often toward the most beautiful of castles, which contained the most beautiful of young baronesses. He lay down without eating supper, between two furrows in an open field; it was snowing in large flakes. The next day, chilled to the bone, he dragged himself to the nearest town, whose name was Waldberghoff-trarbk-dikdorff. Penniless, dying of hunger and fatigue, he stopped sadly in front of an inn. Two men dressed in blue[1] noticed him.

"Comrade," said one of them, "there's a well-built young man who's just the right height."

They went up to Candide and politely asked him to dine with them.

"Gentlemen," said Candide with charming modesty, "I'm deeply honored, but I have no money to pay my share."

"Ah, sir," said one of the men in blue, "people of your appearance and merit never pay anything: aren't you five feet five?"

"Yes, gentlemen, that's my height," he said, bowing.

"Come, sir, sit down. We'll not only pay for your dinner, but we'll never let a man like you be short of money. Men were made only to help each other."

"You're right," said Candide, "that's what Dr. Pangloss always told me, and I see that all is for the best."

They begged him to accept a little money; he took it and offered to sign a note for it, but they would not let him. They all sat down to table.

"Don't you dearly love—"

"Oh, yes!" answered Candide. "I dearly love Lady Cunegonde."

"No," said one of the men, "we want to know if you dearly love the King of the Bulgars."

"Not at all," said Candide, "because I've never seen him."

"What! He's the most charming of kings, and we must drink to his health."

"Oh, I'll be glad to, gentlemen!"

And he drank.

"That's enough," he was told, "you're now the support, the upholder, the defender and the hero of the Bulgars: your fortune is made and your glory is assured."

They immediately put irons on his legs and took him to a regiment. He was taught to make right and left turns, raise and lower the ramrod, take aim, fire, and march double time, and he was beaten thirty times with a stick. The next day he performed his drills a little less badly and was given only twenty strokes; the following day he was given only ten, and his fellow soldiers regarded him as a prodigy.

Candide, utterly bewildered, still could not make

out very clearly how he was a hero. One fine spring day he decided to take a stroll; he walked straight ahead, believing that the free use of the legs was a privilege of both mankind and the animals. He had not gone five miles when four other heroes, all six feet tall, overtook him, bound him, brought him back and put him in a dungeon. With proper legal procedure, he was asked which he would prefer, to be beaten thirty-six times by the whole regiment, or to receive twelve bullets in his brain. It did him no good to maintain that man's will is free and that he wanted neither: he had to make a choice. Using the gift of God known as freedom, he decided to run the gauntlet thirty-six times, and did so twice. The regiment was composed of two thousand men, so his punishment was so far composed of four thousand strokes, which had laid bare every muscle and nerve from his neck to his backside. As they were preparing for a third run, Candide, unable to go on, begged them to blow his brains out instead. The favor was granted; he was blindfolded and made to kneel. Just then the King of the Bulgars came by and inquired about the condemned man's crime. Being a highly intelligent king, he realized from what he was told that Candide was a young metaphysician, utterly ignorant of worldly matters, and pardoned him with a clemency that will be praised in all newspapers and all ages. A worthy surgeon healed Candide in three weeks with the emollients prescribed by Dioscorides. He already had a little skin, and was able to walk, when the King of the Bulgars joined battle with the King of the Avars.

CHAPTER III

*How Candide escaped from the Bulgars,
and what happened to him.*

NOTHING could have been more splendid, brilliant, smart or orderly than the two armies. The trumpets, fifes, oboes, drums and cannons produced a harmony whose equal was never heard in hell. First the cannons laid low about six thousand men on each side, then rifle fire removed from the best of worlds about nine or ten thousand scoundrels who had been infesting its surface. The bayonet was also the sufficient reason for the death of several thousand men. The total may well have risen to thirty thousand souls. Candide, trembling like a philosopher, hid himself as best he could during this heroic carnage.

Finally, while the two kings were having Te Deums sung, each in his own camp, Candide decided to go elsewhere to reason about cause and effect. He made his way over heaps of dead and dying men until he came to a nearby village. It was in ashes, for it was an Avar village which the Bulgars had burned in accordance with international law. Old men with wounds all over their bodies were watching the death throes of butchered women who clutched their children to their bloody breasts; girls who had been disemboweled after satisfying the natural needs of several heroes were breathing their last sighs; others, mortally burned, were shrieking for someone to hasten their death. The ground was strewn with brains and severed arms and legs.

Candide fled to another village as fast as he could: it belonged to the Bulgars, and the Avar heroes had treated it in the same manner. Still walking over quivering limbs, or through ruins, he finally emerged from the theater of war, carrying a little food in his sack and never forgetting Lady Cunegonde. His food ran out when he reached Holland, but since he had heard that everyone was rich in that country, and that the people were Christians, he did not doubt that he would be treated as well there as he had been in the baron's castle before he had been driven away from it because of Lady Cunegonde's lovely eyes.

He asked alms of several solemn individuals who all replied that if he continued to ply that trade he would be shut up in a house of correction to teach him better manners.

Next he approached a man who had just spoken

about charity for a whole hour in front of a large assembly. This orator scowled at him and said, "What are you doing here? Are you for the good cause?"

"There is no effect without a cause," replied Candide modestly. "All things are necessarily connected and arranged for the best. I had to be driven away from Lady Cunegonde, I had to run the gauntlet, and I have to beg my bread until I can earn it; all that could not have been otherwise."

"My friend," said the orator, "do you believe that the Pope is the Antichrist?"

"I've never heard anyone say so," answered Candide, "but whether he is or not, I still have nothing to eat."

"You don't deserve to eat," said the orator. "Go, you scoundrel, you wretch, and never come near me again!"

The orator's wife, having looked out the window and seen a man who doubted that the Pope was the Antichrist, poured on his head the contents of a full . . . O heaven! To what excesses are ladies driven by religious zeal!

A man who had not been baptized, a good Anabaptist by the name of James, witnessed this cruel and ignominious treatment of one of his fellow men, a featherless biped who had a soul; he took him to his home, washed him, served him bread and beer, made him a gift of two florins and even offered to teach him to work for him in the manufacture of those Persian fabrics that are produced in Holland. Candide almost threw himself at his feet. "Dr. Pangloss was right when he told me that all is for the best in this world," he said, "because your extreme generosity has moved me much more deeply than the harshness of that gentleman in the black cloak and his wife."

The next day, as he was taking a walk he met a beggar covered with sores; his eyes were lifeless, the tip of his nose had been eaten away, his mouth was twisted, his teeth were black, his voice was hoarse, he was racked by a violent cough, and he spat out a tooth with every spasm.

CHAPTER IV

How Candide met his former philosophy teacher, Dr. Pangloss, and what ensued.

CANDIDE, moved even more by compassion than by horror, gave this appalling beggar the two florins he had received from James, the worthy Anabaptist. The apparition stared at him, shed tears and threw his arms around his neck. Candide drew back in terror.

"Alas," said one pauper to the other, "don't you recognize your dear Pangloss?"

"What are you saying! You, my dear master! You, in this horrible condition! What misfortune has befallen you? Why are you no longer in the most beautiful of castles? What has become of Lady Cunegonde, the pearl of young ladies, the masterpiece of nature?"

"I'm at the end of my strength," said Pangloss.

Candide immediately took him to the Anabaptist's stable, where he gave him a little bread to eat, and when he had revived he said to him, "Well, what about Cunegonde?"

"She's dead," replied Pangloss.

Candide fainted at this word; his friend brought him back to consciousness with some bad vinegar that happened to be in the stable. Candide opened his eyes and said, "Cunegonde is dead! Oh, best of all possible worlds, where are you? But what did she die of? Was it from seeing me kicked out of the beautiful castle by her father?"

"No," said Pangloss, "she was disemboweled by Bulgar soldiers after having been raped as much as a woman can be. They smashed the baron's head when he tried to defend her, the baroness was hacked to pieces, and my poor pupil was treated exactly the same as his sister. As for the castle, not one stone was left standing on another; there's not one barn left, not one sheep, not one duck, not one tree. But we were well avenged, because the Avars did the same thing to a nearby estate that belonged to a Bulgar lord."

At this account, Candide fainted again; but, when he had regained his senses and said everything required by the situation, he inquired into cause and effect, and the sufficient reason that had reduced Pangloss to such a pitiful state.

"Alas," said Pangloss, "it was love: love, the consoler of the human race, the preserver of the universe, the soul of all sensitive beings, tender love."

"Alas," said Candide, "I too have known love, that ruler of hearts, that soul of our soul: it's never brought me anything except one kiss and twenty kicks in the rump. How could such a beautiful cause produce such an abominable effect on you?"

Pangloss answered in these terms: "My dear Candide, you knew Paquette, our noble baroness's pretty maid; in her arms I tasted the delights of paradise, and they produced these torments of hell with which you see me devoured: she was infected with them, and by now she may have died of them. It was a present given to her by a learned Franciscan friar who had derived it from the point of origin, for it was given to him by an old countess, who received it from a cavalry captain, who owed it to a marquise, who got it from a page, who was given it by a Jesuit who, while still a novice, had received it in a direct line from a shipmate of Christopher Columbus. As for me, I won't give it to anyone, because I'm dying."

"Oh, Pangloss!" cried Candide. "What a strange genealogy! Didn't it begin with the devil?"

"Not at all," replied the great man. "It was an indispensable element in the best of worlds, a necessary ingredient, because if Columbus, on an American island, hadn't caught that disease which poisons the source of generation, which often even prevents generation, and which is obviously opposed to the great goal of nature, we would now have neither chocolate nor cochineal. It must also be noted that so far, on our continent, this disease is peculiar to us, like religious controversy. The Turks, Indians, Persians,

Chinese, Siamese and Japanese are still unacquainted with it; but there's a sufficient reason for their also coming to know it within a few centuries. Meanwhile, it's made amazing progress among us, especially in those great armies, composed of honest and well-bred mercenaries, which decide the fate of nations: it can safely be said that whenever thirty thousand men fight a pitched battle against an equal number of enemy troops, there are about twenty thousand syphilitics on each side."

"That's admirable," said Candide, "but you must be cured."

"How can I be?" said Pangloss. "I'm penniless, my friend, and nowhere on the face of the globe can you get a blood letting or an enema without paying, or having someone pay for you."

This statement decided Candide: he went back to James, the charitable Anabaptist, threw himself at his feet and painted such a heart-rending picture of the state to which his friend had been reduced that the good man did not hesitate to take Dr. Pangloss into his house and have him cured at his expense. When his treatment was over, Pangloss had lost only an eye and an ear. He could write well and knew arithmetic perfectly. The Anabaptist made him his bookkeeper. Two months later he was obliged to go to Lisbon on business; he took the two philosophers with him on his ship. Pangloss explained to him how all was for the very best. James did not share this opinion.

"Men," he said, "must have corrupted nature a little, because they weren't born wolves, yet they've become wolves: God didn't give them twenty-four-pounders or bayonets, but they've made themselves bayonets and cannons with which to destroy each other. I might also mention bankruptcies, and the law which takes over a bankrupt's property to defraud his creditors of it."

"All that was indispensable," replied the one-eyed doctor, "and individual misfortunes create general welfare, so that the more individual misfortunes there are, the more all is well."

While he was reasoning thus, the air grew dark, the winds blew from the four corners of the earth, and the ship was assailed by a terrible storm in sight of the port of Lisbon.

CHAPTER V

Storm, shipwreck and earthquake, and what happened to Dr. Pangloss, Candide and James the Anabaptist.

HALF the passengers, expiring from the indescribable agony which the rolling of a ship inflicts on the nerves and humors of the body, shaken in different directions, were so weakened that they lacked even the strength to become alarmed at their danger. The other half were shrieking and praying. The sails were torn, the masts were broken, the hull was cracked open. Those who could work were doing so, but they were all at cross-purposes because no one was in command. The Anabaptist was topside, helping a little to handle the ship. A frenzied sailor struck him violently and laid him out flat on the deck, but his own blow threw him off balance and he fell overboard, head first. He was caught on part of a broken mast and remained hanging there. The good James rushed to his assistance and helped him climb back on board, but, in the course of his efforts, he was thrown into the sea in full view of the sailor, who let him perish without deigning even to look at him. Candide came over and saw his benefactor reappear on the surface for a moment before sinking forever. He tried to leap into the sea after him; Pangloss the philosopher stopped him by proving to him that the Lisbon harbor was formed expressly for the Anabaptist to drown in. As he was proving this *a priori*, the ship split open and everyone perished except Pangloss, Candide and the brutal sailor who had drowned the virtuous Anabaptist; the scoundrel easily swam to land, and Pangloss and Candide were carried ashore on a plank.

When they had recovered a little, they walked toward Lisbon. They still had some money left, with which they hoped to save themselves from starvation, after having escaped from the storm.

They had scarcely set foot in the city, mourning the death of their benefactor, when they felt the earth tremble[2] beneath them. The sea boiled up in the harbor and smashed the vessels lying at anchor. Whirlwinds of flame and ashes covered the streets and squares, houses collapsed, roofs were thrown onto foundations and the foundations crumbled; thirty thousand inhabitants of all ages and both sexes were crushed beneath the ruins.

The sailor whistled, swore and said, "I'll get something out of this."

"What can be the sufficient reason for this phenomenon?" said Pangloss.

"This is the end of the world!" cried Candide.

The sailor immediately rushed into the midst of the wreckage, braved death to find money, found some, took it with him, got drunk and, after sobering up a little, bought the favors of the first willing girl he met in the ruins of the destroyed houses, amid the dead and dying. But Pangloss pulled him by the sleeve and said to him, "You're behaving badly, my friend: you're not respecting universal reason, you've chosen a bad time for this."

"By the blood of Christ! I'm a sailor and I was born in Batavia: I've walked on the crucifix four times during four stays in Japan—you've come to the right man with your universal reason!"

Candide had been wounded by several splinters of stone. He was lying in the street, covered with rubble. He said to Pangloss, "Alas! Get me some wine and oil: I'm dying."

"This earthquake is nothing new," replied Pangloss. "The town of Lima in America felt the same shocks last year. Same causes, same effects; there is surely a vein of sulphur running underground from Lima to Lisbon."

"Nothing is more likely," said Candide, "but, in the name of God, bring me some oil and wine!"

"What do you mean, likely?" retorted the philosopher. "I maintain that the fact is demonstrated."

Candide lost consciousness, and Pangloss brought him a little water from a nearby fountain.

The next day, having found a little food as they slipped through the ruins, they recovered some of their strength. Then they worked like the others to help those inhabitants who had escaped death. Some of the citizens they assisted gave them as good a dinner as was possible in such a disaster. The meal was sad, it is true. The hosts wet their bread with their tears, but Pangloss comforted them by assuring them that things could not have been otherwise: "For," he said, "all is for the best. For if there's a volcano at Lisbon, it couldn't be anywhere else. For it's impossible for things not to be where they are. For all is well."

A little man in black, an officer of the Inquisition, who was sitting beside him, spoke up politely and said, "Apparently you don't believe in original sin, sir; *for* if all is for the best, there can be no fall or punishment."

"I humbly beg Your Excellency's pardon," replied Pangloss still more politely, "for the fall of man, and his curse, were necessary components of the best of all possible worlds."

"Then you don't believe in free will, sir?" said the officer.

"Excuse me, Your Excellency," said Pangloss, "but freedom can subsist with absolute necessity, for it was necessary that we be free; for, after all, a determined will—"

Pangloss was in the middle of his sentence when the officer nodded to his armed attendant, who was pouring him out a glass of port, or Oporto wine.

CHAPTER VI

How a fine auto-da-fé was performed to prevent earthquakes, and how Candide was flogged.

AFTER the earthquake had destroyed three-quarters of Lisbon, the wise men of the country could think of no more effective way of avoiding total ruin than giving the populace a fine auto-da-fé. It was decided by the University of Coimbra that the sight of several people being slowly burned with great ceremony was an infallible means of preventing the earth from quaking.

They had therefore arrested a Biscayan convicted of marrying the godmother of his godchild, and two Portuguese who had taken the pork from the outside of their chicken before eating it; and, after dinner, Dr. Pangloss and his disciple Candide were bound and taken away, one for having spoken, the other for having listened with an air of approval. They were separated and each was placed in an extremely cool room where no one was ever bothered by the sun. A week later they were both dressed in sanbenitos and paper miters. Candide's miter and sanbenito bore painted flames, pointed downward, and devils without tails or claws; but Pangloss's devils had claws and tails, and his flames were upright. Thus attired, they walked in a procession and heard a deeply moving sermon, followed by beautiful polyphonic music. Candide was flogged in time with the singing, the Biscayan and the two men who had refused to eat pork were burned, and Pangloss was hanged, although this was not customary. That same day the earth shook again, with a terrible uproar.

Terrified, bewildered, frantic, covered with blood, quivering all over, Candide said to himself, "If this is the best of all possible worlds, what are the others like? I wouldn't complain if it were just that I'd been flogged: the Bulgars flogged me too. But my dear Pangloss, the greatest of philosophers—did I have to see you hanged, without knowing why? And my dear Anabaptist, the kindest of men—did you have to be drowned in the harbor? And Lady Cunegonde, the pearl of young ladies—did your belly have to be slit open?"

He was just beginning to walk away, having been preached at, flogged, absolved and blessed, when an old woman accosted him and said, "Cheer up, my son. Follow me."

CHAPTER VII

How an old woman took care of Candide, and how he found the object of his love.

CANDIDE did not cheer up, but he did follow the old woman into a hovel. She gave him a jar of ointment to rub on himself and set out food and drink for him; then she showed him a rather clean little bed with a suit of clothes beside it. "Eat, drink and sleep," she said to him, "and may Our Lady of Atocha, My Lord Saint Anthony of Padua and My Lord Saint James of Compostella take care of you. I'll come back tomorrow."

Candide, still amazed by everything he had seen and suffered, and even more amazed by the old woman's kindness, tried to kiss her hand, but she said to him, "It's not *my* hand you should kiss. I'll come back tomorrow. Rub yourself with ointment, eat and sleep."

Despite all his misfortunes, Candide ate and slept. The next morning the old woman brought him some breakfast, examined his back and rubbed it herself with another kind of ointment. She later brought him dinner, then came back in the evening with supper. The following day she rendered him the same services.

"Who are you?" Candide kept asking her. "Why are you so kind to me? What can I do to show my gratitude?"

The good woman never answered. She came back that evening, but she brought no supper.

"Come with me," she said, "and don't say a word."

She took him by the arm and they walked out of town about a quarter of a mile until they came to an isolated house surrounded by gardens and rectangular ponds. The old woman knocked at a little door. It opened; she led Candide up a concealed staircase and into a gilded room, left him on a brocaded couch, shut the door and went away. He thought he must be dreaming; he regarded his whole life as a nightmare, and the present moment as a delightful vision.

The old woman soon returned. She was supporting with difficulty a trembling woman with a majestic figure, glittering with precious stones and covered by a veil.

"Lift her veil," the old woman said to Candide.

The young man stepped forward and timidly lifted the veil. What a moment! What a surprise! He thought he saw Lady Cunegonde—he actually did see her, it was she herself! His strength failed him, he was unable to say a word; he fell at her feet. She fell on the couch. The old woman plied them with spirits until they returned to their senses. They spoke to each other: at first there were only broken words, simultaneous questions and answers, sighs, tears and exclamations. The old woman urged them to make less noise and left them alone together.

"What! Is it really you?" said Candide. "You're still alive! I've found you again in Portugal! So you weren't raped? Your belly wasn't slit open, as Pangloss the philosopher assured me?"

"He was right," said the fair Cunegonde, "but those two accidents aren't always fatal."

"But weren't your parents killed?"

"It's all too true," said Cunegonde, weeping.

"And what about your brother?"

"He was also killed."

"And why are you in Portugal, and how did you find out I was here, and through what strange adventure did you have me brought here?"

"I'll tell you all that," replied the lady, "but first you must tell me everything that's happened to you since the innocent kiss you gave me, and the kicks you received."

Candide obeyed her with deep respect; although he was still in a daze, although his voice was weak and quivering, and although his spine was still aching, he related in a perfectly natural manner everything he had experienced since their parting. Cunegonde raised her eyes to heaven, shedding tears over the death of the good Anabaptist and Pangloss. Then she spoke to Candide as follows, while he hung on her every word and devoured her with his eyes.

CHAPTER VIII

Cunegonde's story.

I was in my bed, sleeping soundly, when it pleased heaven to send the Bulgars to our beautiful castle of Thunder-ten-tronckh. They butchered my father and brother, and cut my mother to pieces. A big, six-foot Bulgar saw that I'd fainted at the sight and began raping me. That brought me back to my senses; I screamed, struggled, bit, clawed and tried to scratch his eyes out, not knowing that everything happening in my father's castle was quite customary. The brute stabbed me in the left side; I still have the scar."

"Oh! I hope I'll see it!" exclaimed the naïve Candide.

"You will," said Cunegonde, "but let me go on."

"Please do," said Candide.

She resumed her story: "A Bulgar captain came in and saw the blood streaming from me. The soldier paid no attention to him. The brute's lack of respect for him made the captain angry, so he killed him while he was still on me. Then he had my wounds dressed and took me to his quarters as a prisoner of war. I washed the few shirts he had, and did his cooking. I must confess that he found me very pretty, and I won't deny that he was a handsome, well-built man with soft, white skin. But he had little intelligence and knew little about philosophy; it was easy to see that he hadn't been brought up by Dr. Pangloss. Three months later, he'd lost all his money and become tired of me, so he sold me to Don Issachar, a Jew who traded in Holland and Portugal and was passionately fond of women. Don Issachar took a great liking to my person, but he was unable to triumph over it: I resisted him better than I had the Bulgar soldier. A lady of honor may be raped once, but it strengthens her virtue. To make me more compliant, he brought me to this country house. Till then, I'd thought there was nothing on earth so beautiful as the castle of Thunder-ten-tronckh. I saw that I was wrong.

"One day the Grand Inquisitor noticed me at mass. He stared at me for a long time and sent word to me that he had some secret matters to discuss with me. I was taken to his palace. I told him of my birth, and he pointed out to me how degrading it was for a lady of my rank to belong to an Israelite. It was then suggested to Don Issachar that he should cede me to His Eminence. Don Issachar, who's the court banker and a man of influence, flatly refused. The Inquisitor threatened him with an auto-da-fé. Finally Don Issachar, intimidated, made a bargain whereby the house and I belong to both of them in common: to him on Mondays, Wednesdays and the Sabbath, and to the Inquisitor on the other days of the week. The agreement has been in effect for six months now, but not without quarrels, because it's often been undecided whether the night between Saturday and Sunday belongs to the old law or the new. For my part, I've resisted them both so far, and I think that's why I've always been loved.

"Finally, to ward off the scourge of earthquakes and intimidate Don Issachar, the Inquisitor decided to celebrate an auto-da-fé. He did me the honor of inviting me to attend it. I had a very good seat; refreshments were served to the ladies between the mass and the executions. To tell you the truth, I was horrified when I saw them burn those two Jews and that honest Biscayan who had married the godmother of his godchild; but imagine my surprise, my terror, my agitation, when I saw a man who looked like Pangloss, wearing a sanbenito and a miter! I rubbed my eyes and looked carefully. I saw him hanged. I fainted. I'd scarcely recovered when I saw you stripped naked; I was overcome with horror, consternation, sorrow and despair. Let me tell you truthfully that your skin is even whiter than my Bulgar captain's, and has a more perfect bloom. This sight doubled all the emotions that were crushing me, consuming me. I cried out, I tried to say 'Stop, barbarians!' but my voice failed me; anyway, my cries would have been useless. When you'd been thoroughly flogged, I said to myself, 'How can it be that the charming Candide and the wise Pangloss have come to Lisbon, one to receive a hundred lashes, the other to be hanged by order of His Eminence the Inquisitor, who loves me dearly? I see now that Pangloss cruelly deceived me when he told me that all was for the best in this world.'

"I was agitated and frantic, sometimes beside myself, sometimes ready to die of faintness, and my mind was filled with the slaughter of my parents and my brother, the insolence of that horrible Bulgar soldier, the knife wound he gave me, my servitude, my work as a cook, my Bulgar captain, my horrible Don Issachar, my abominable Inquisitor, the hanging of Dr. Pangloss, that great Miserere during which you were flogged, and, above all, the kiss you gave me behind a screen when I saw you for the last time. I praised God for bringing you back to me through so many ordeals. I told my old servant to take care of you and bring you here as soon as she could. She's carried out my orders very well; I've known the inexpressible joy of seeing you again, of hearing you and talking to you. You must be ravenously hungry; I have a good appetite too, so let's begin by eating supper."

They sat down to table together, and after supper they returned to the beautiful couch that has already been mentioned. They were still on it when Don Issachar, one of the masters of the house, arrived. It was the day of the Sabbath. He had come to enjoy his rights and express his tender love.

CHAPTER IX

What happened to Cunegonde, Candide, the Grand Inquisitor and the Jew.

THIS Issachar was the most irascible Hebrew that had been seen in Israel since the Babylonian captivity. "What!" he cried. "Isn't the Inquisitor enough, you Galilean bitch? Must this scoundrel share you with me too?" So saying, he took out a long dagger which he always had on him, and, thinking his adversary was unarmed, threw himself on Candide. But our good Westphalian had received a fine sword with the suit of clothes the old woman had given him. Despite his gentle nature, he drew this sword and laid the Israelite out on the floor, dead as a doornail, at the feet of the fair Cunegonde.

"Holy Virgin!" she cried. "What will become of us? A man killed in my house! If the police come, we're lost!"

"If Pangloss hadn't been hanged," said Candide, "he'd give us good advice in this extremity, because he was a great philosopher. Lacking him, let's consult the old woman."

She was extremely prudent, and she was beginning to give her opinion when another little door opened. It was an hour past midnight: Sunday had begun, and that day belonged to the Inquisitor. He came in and saw the flogged Candide with a sword in his hand, a dead man stretched out on the floor, Cunegonde in a state of panic, and the old woman giving advice.

This is what went through Candide's mind at that moment, and how he reasoned: "If this holy man calls for help, he'll certainly have me burned, and he may

do the same thing to Cunegonde. He's had me whipped unmercifully. He's my rival. I've already begun killing: my course is clear." This reasoning was swift and sure; without giving the Inquisitor time to recover from his surprise, he ran him through and laid him out beside the Jew.

"Now we're in an even worse predicament!" said Cunegonde. "They'll have no mercy on us. We'll be excommunicated, our last hour has come. How could a gentle man like you kill a Jew and a prelate within two minutes of each other?"

"Fairest lady," said Candide, "when a man is in love, jealous, and whipped by the Inquisition, he no longer knows what he's doing."

At this point the old woman spoke up: "There are three Andalusian horses in the stable, with saddles and bridles: brave Candide must get them ready. Madam has some gold coins and diamonds. Let's mount the horses without delay, although I can sit on only one buttock, and ride to Cadiz. The weather is perfect, and it's very pleasant to travel in the cool of the night."

Candide immediately saddled the three horses. He, Cunegonde and the old woman covered thirty miles without stopping. As they were riding away, the Holy Brotherhood came into the house. His Eminence was buried in a beautiful church, and Issachar was thrown into the garbage dump.

Candide, Cunegonde and the old woman had already reached the little town of Avacena in the middle of the Sierra Morena, and they were speaking as follows in an inn.

CHAPTER X

*How Candide, Cunegonde and the old woman
arrived at Cadiz in great distress, and how
they set sail from there.*

W HO could have stolen my money and diamonds?"
said Cunegonde, weeping. "What are we going to live
on? What shall we do? Where will I find Inquisitors
and Jews who will give me more money and diamonds?"

"Alas," said the old woman, "I strongly suspect a
reverend Franciscan who slept in the same inn with
us last night in Badajoz; God preserve me from making a rash judgment, but he did come into our room
twice, and he left the inn long before we did."

"Alas," said Candide, "my dear Pangloss often
proved to me that the goods of this world are common
to all men, that everyone has an equal right to them.
Acting on that principle, the Franciscan should have
left us enough to finish our· journey. So you have
nothing left, fair Cunegonde?"

"Not a penny," she said.

"What shall we do?" said Candide.

"Let's sell one of the horses," said the old woman.
"I'll ride behind Madam, although I can sit only on
one buttock, and we'll go on to Cadiz."

There was a Benedictine prior staying at the same
inn. He bought the horse for a low price. Candide,
Cunegonde and the old woman went through Lucena,
Chillas and Lebrija, and finally reached Cadiz. A fleet
was being fitted out there, and troops were being
assembled to bring the reverend Jesuit fathers of
Paraguay to reason, for they had been accused of in-
citing their tribes near the town of Sacramento to
revolt against the King of Spain and the King of
Portugal. Candide, having served in a Bulgar regiment, went through the Bulgar drills in front of the

general of the little army with such grace, speed, skill, pride and agility that he was placed in command of a company of infantry. Now that he was a captain, he boarded a ship with Lady Cunegonde, the old woman, two menservants, and the two Andalusian horses that had once belonged to the Grand Inquisitor of Portugal.

During the whole voyage they often discussed poor Pangloss's philosophy. "We're going to another world," said Candide. "It must be the one in which all is well, because I must admit that it's possible to complain about some of the things that go on in our world, from both a physical and a moral point of view."

"I love you with all my heart," said Cunegonde, "but my soul is still shocked by what I've seen and experienced."

"Everything will go well," replied Candide. "I've already noticed that the sea of this New World is better than our European seas: it's calmer, and the winds are steadier. I'm sure it's the New World that's the best of all possible worlds."

"May God grant that you're right!" said Cunegonde. "But I've had such horrible misfortunes in my world that my heart is nearly closed to hope."

"You both complain," said the old woman, "but neither of you has known misfortunes like mine."

Cunegonde nearly laughed: she found it amusing of the old servant to claim to have been more unfortunate than she. "My good woman," she said, "unless you've been raped by two Bulgars, been stabbed in the belly twice, seen two of your castles demolished, had two mothers and two fathers murdered before your eyes, and seen two of your lovers flogged in an auto-da-fé, I don't see how you can surpass me; and let me add that I was born a baroness with seventy-two generations of nobility, and then became a cook."

"Madam," replied the old woman, "you don't know about my birth, and if I were to show you my backside you wouldn't talk that way: you'd suspend judgment."

These remarks aroused intense curiosity in the minds of Cunegonde and Candide. The old woman spoke to them as follows.

CHAPTER XI

The old woman's story.

My eyes haven't always been bloodshot and redrimmed, my nose hasn't always touched my chin, and I haven't always been a servant. I am the daughter of Pope Urban X and the Princess of Palestrina.[3] Until the age of fourteen I was brought up in a palace so magnificent that all the castles of your German barons couldn't have served as its stable, and one of my dresses was worth more than all the splendor in Westphalia. I grew in beauty, grace and talent, amid pleasures, respect and hopes. I had already begun to inspire love. My breasts were forming, and what breasts! They were white and firm, and as shapely as those of the Venus de' Medici. And what eyes I had! What eyelids! What black eyebrows! What fire shone from my two pupils, dimming the glitter of the stars, as the local poets used to tell me! The women who dressed and undressed me were ecstatic each time they saw me in front and behind, and all men would have loved to be in their place.

"I was betrothed to a sovereign prince of Massa-Carrara. What a prince! He was as handsome as I was beautiful, filled with sweetness and charm, sparkling with wit and burning with love. I loved him as we always love the first time: with idolatry and wild passion. Preparations for the wedding were made with unprecedented pomp and splendor: there were constant feasts, tournaments and comic operas, and all Italy wrote sonnets for me, not one of which was even passable. I was about to reach the peak of my happiness when an old marchesa who'd once been my prince's mistress invited him to her house for choco-

42

late. He died in less than two hours, with horrible convulsions. But that's only a trifle. My mother, in despair, though less deeply afflicted than I, decided to leave the tragic scene for a while. She had a beautiful estate near Gaeta. We set out in a galley that was gilded like the altar of St. Peter's in Rome. Suddenly a Barbary pirate ship bore down on us and boarded us. Our soldiers defended themselves like soldiers of the pope: they all knelt, threw down their arms and asked the pirates for absolution *in articulo mortis*.

"They were immediately stripped as naked as monkeys, and so were my mother, our ladies-in-waiting and I. It's amazing how quickly those gentlemen can undress people. But what surprised me even more was that they put their fingers in a place where we women usually allow nothing but the nozzle of an enema. This ceremony seemed very strange to me; that's how we judge everything when we've never been outside our own country before. I soon learned that it was to find out whether we'd hidden any diamonds there. It's a custom that's been observed since time immemorial by all civilized seafaring nations. I later learned that the Knights of Malta never fail to practice it when they capture Turkish men and women. It's a point of international law which has always been complied with.

"I won't tell you how painful it is for a young princess to be taken off to Morocco as a slave with her mother. You can easily imagine everything we had to suffer on board the pirate ship. My mother was still quite beautiful; our ladies-in-waiting and even our ordinary maids had more charms than can be found in all of Africa. As for me, I was exquisitely lovely; I was beauty and grace personified, and I was a virgin. Not for long, though: the flower that had been reserved for the handsome Prince of Massa-Carrara was ravished from me by the pirate captain, a horrible Negro who thought he was doing me a great honor. The Princess of Palestrina and I certainly needed all our strength to withstand everything we underwent before we reached Morocco. But I won't dwell on that;

such things are so common that they're not worth talking about.

"Morocco was swimming in blood when we arrived. There were fifty sons of the Emperor Muley Ismael, each with his own faction; this produced fifty civil wars, of blacks against blacks, blacks against browns, browns against browns, and mulattoes against mulattoes. There was constant slaughter from one end of the empire to the other.

"We had scarcely landed when some blacks belonging to an enemy faction attacked my pirate captain to take his booty away from him. After the diamonds and gold, we were his most valuable prizes. I witnessed a fight such as you never see in our European climates. Northern peoples aren't hot-blooded enough. Their lust for women isn't as strong as it usually is in Africa. Europeans seem to have milk in their veins, but it's fire and vitriol that flows in the veins of those who live in the Atlas Mountains and the surrounding regions. They fought with the fury of the lions, tigers and snakes of their country to decide who would have us. A Moor seized my mother by the right arm, my captain's lieutenant held her by the left, a Moorish soldier took her by one leg, and one of our pirates gripped the other. Nearly all our women were instantly seized and drawn this way by four soldiers. My captain kept me hidden behind him. He had his scimitar in his hand and was killing everyone who faced his rage. Finally I saw my mother and all our Italian women torn and cut to pieces, slaughtered by the monsters who were fighting over them. My fellow captives and those who had captured them—soldiers, sailors, blacks, whites, mulattoes, and finally my captain—were all killed, and I lay dying on a heap of corpses. As you know, such scenes took place all over an area seven hundred fifty miles across, yet no one ever missed the five daily prayers prescribed by Mohammed.

"I freed myself with great difficulty from that tangled mass of bleeding corpses and dragged myself to the shade of a big orange tree on the bank of a nearby

44

stream. I collapsed there, overcome with fear, fatigue, horror, despair and hunger. My exhausted senses soon sank into an oblivion that was more like fainting than sleeping. I was in that state of weakness and insensibility, between life and death, when I felt something moving and pressing against my body. I opened my eyes and saw a white man of good appearance who was sighing and muttering between his teeth, '*O che sciagùra d'essere senza coglioni!*⁴' "

CHAPTER XII

Further misfortunes of the old woman.

Astonished and delighted to hear the language of my country, and equally surprised by the words the man was saying, I replied to him that there were greater misfortunes than the one he was complaining of. I gave him a brief account of the horrors I had gone through, then fainted again. He carried me to a nearby house, had me put in bed and given something to eat, waited on me, comforted me, caressed me and told me he'd never seen anything so beautiful as I, and that never before had he so keenly regretted the loss of what no one could give back to him.

" 'I was born in Naples,' he said, 'where they castrate two or three thousand children every year. Some of them die of it, others acquire more beautiful voices than that of any woman, still others go off to rule states. In my case, the operation was a great success, and I became a musician in the chapel of the Princess of Palestrina.'

" 'My mother's chapel!' I cried.

" 'Your mother?' he exclaimed, weeping. 'What! Are you that young princess I brought up to the age of six, and who even then showed promise of becoming as beautiful as you are now?'

" 'Yes, I am. My mother is only four hundred yards

from here, cut into quarters and lying under a heap of corpses.'

"I told him everything that had happened to me, and he also related his adventures. He told me how he had been sent to the King of Morocco by a Christian power to make a treaty with that monarch whereby he would be supplied with gunpowder, cannons and ships to help him wipe out the trade of other Christian powers.

"'My mission is accomplished,' said the honest eunuch, 'and I'm going to set sail from Ceuta. I'll take you back to Italy with me. *Ma che sciagùra d'essere senza coglioni!*'

"I thanked him with tears of gratitude in my eyes. Instead of taking me back to Italy, he took me to Algiers and sold me to the dey of that province. I'd scarcely been sold when the plague that swept over Africa, Asia and Europe broke out violently in Algiers. You've seen earthquakes, Madam, but have you ever had the plague?"

"Never," replied the baroness.

"If you had," said the old woman, "you'd admit that it's much worse than an earthquake. It's very common in Africa; I caught it. Imagine the situation of a pope's daughter, fifteen years old, who, in the space of three months, had undergone poverty and slavery, been raped almost every day, seen her mother cut into quarters, experienced hunger and war, and was now dying of the plague in Algiers. I didn't die, however, but my eunuch, the dey, and nearly the whole harem of Algiers perished.

"When the first ravages of that terrible plague had passed, the dey's slaves were sold. A trader bought me and took me to Tunis. He sold me to another trader, who sold me in Tripoli; I was sold again in Alexandria, then in Smyrna, then in Constantinople. Finally I belonged to an aga of the Janizaries, who was soon sent to defend Azov against the besieging Russians.

"The aga, a very gallant man, took his whole harem with him and lodged us in a little fort on the shore of the Sea of Azov, where we were guarded by two

Negro eunuchs and twenty soldiers. Prodigious numbers of Russians were killed, but they gave back as much as they took. Azov was burned and there was a general massacre, without regard for sex or age. Only our little fort was left. The enemy tried to starve us out. The twenty Janizaries had sworn never to surrender. The extremities of hunger to which they were reduced forced them to eat our two eunuchs, for fear of breaking their oath. Several days later, they decided to eat the women.

"There was a very pious and compassionate Moslem chaplain with us; he preached a beautiful sermon to them in which he persuaded them not to kill us completely. 'Cut off only one buttock from each of these ladies,' he said, 'and you'll have a delicious meal. If you need more, you can have the same amount again in several days. Heaven will be pleased by such a charitable action, and help will be brought to you.'

"He was very eloquent, and he convinced them. We underwent that horrible operation. The chaplain treated us with the same ointment that's used on children who've just been circumcised. We were all nearly dead.

"Soon after the Janizaries had finished the meal we'd provided, the Russians arrived in flatboats. Not one Janizary escaped. The Russians paid no attention to the state we were in. There are French surgeons everywhere; one of them, a very skillful man, took care of us and cured us, and I'll never forget how he made propositions to me as soon as my wounds were healed. He also told us not to be downhearted. He assured us that such things had happened during a number of sieges, and that it was one of the rules of war.

"As soon as my companions could walk, they were sent to Moscow. I was taken over by a Boyar as his share of the spoils. He made me his gardener and gave me twenty lashes a day. Two years later, he and about thirty other Boyars were broken on the wheel as the result of a court intrigue. I took advantage of the incident to escape, and I crossed all of Russia. For a long time I was a barmaid in Riga, then in Rostock,

Wismar, Leipzig, Kassel, Utrecht, Leiden, the Hague and Rotterdam. I've grown old in poverty and shame, with only half a behind, always remembering that I'm a pope's daughter. I've wanted to kill myself a hundred times, but I still love life. That ridiculous weakness is perhaps one of our most pernicious inclinations. What could be more stupid than to persist in carrying a burden that we constantly want to cast off, to hold our existence in horror, yet cling to it nonetheless, to fondle the serpent that devours us, until it has eaten our heart?

"In the countries where fate has led me, and in the inns where I've worked, I've seen vast numbers of people who loathed their lives, but I've seen only twelve who voluntarily put an end to their misery: three Negroes, four Englishmen, three Genevans and a German professor named Robeck. I finally became a servant in Don Issachar's house; he placed me in your service, fair lady, I became attached to your destiny, and since then I've been more concerned with your adventures than my own. I'd never have even mentioned my misfortunes to you if you hadn't irked me a little, and if it weren't customary to tell stories on board a ship to while away the time. In short, Madam, I'm a woman of experience, and I know the world. Just for the sake of amusement, ask each passenger to tell you his story, and if you find a single one who hasn't often cursed his life, who hasn't often told himself he was the most miserable man in the world, you can throw me overboard head first."

CHAPTER XIII

How Candide was forced to leave the fair Cunegonde and the old woman.

AFTER hearing the old woman's story, the fair Cunegonde treated her with all the respect due to a person of her rank and merit. Accepting her proposal, she asked all the passengers, one after another, to relate their adventures. She and Candide admitted that the old woman was right.

"It's a great pity," said Candide, "that the wise Pangloss was hanged, contrary to custom, in an auto-da-fé: he would have told us admirable things about the physical and moral evils that cover the earth and the sea, and I would have felt strong enough to venture a few respectful objections."

As each passenger told his story, the ship continued to advance. They landed at Buenos Aires. Cunegonde, Captain Candide and the old woman called on the governor, Don Fernando de Ibaraa, y Figueora, y Mascarenes, y Lampurdos, y Suza. This great lord had the pride befitting a man who bore so many names. He spoke to people with the noblest disdain; he carried his nose so high, raised his voice so mercilessly, adopted such an imposing tone and affected such a haughty bearing that everyone who greeted him was tempted to hit him. He had a furious lust for women. Cunegonde seemed to him the most beautiful woman he had ever seen. The first thing he did was to ask if she was the captain's wife. Candide was alarmed by the way he asked this question. He did not dare say she was his wife, because in fact she was not; he did not dare say she was his sister, because she was not that either, and, although this little white lie was once quite fashionable among the ancients and can still be useful to the moderns, his soul was too pure to betray the truth. "Lady Cunegonde," he said, "will soon do me the honor of becoming my wife, and we beg Your Excellency to be so kind as to celebrate our wedding."

Don Fernando de Ibaraa, y Figueora, y Mascarenes, y Lampurdos, y Suza stroked his mustache, smiled malevolently and ordered Captain Candide to go off and inspect his troops. Candide obeyed, and the governor remained with Lady Cunegonde. He declared his passion to her and vowed he would marry her the next day, in the Church or otherwise, however it might please her charms. Cunegonde asked for a quarter of an hour in which to collect her thoughts, consult the old woman and make up her mind.

The old woman said to her, "Madam, you have seventy-two generations of nobility, but not one penny. You now have a chance to become the wife of a man who's the greatest lord in South America and has a very handsome mustache. Are you in any position to pride yourself on your unshakable fidelity? You've been raped by the Bulgars, and a Jew and an Inquisitor have enjoyed your favors. Misfortune gives us certain rights. I confess that if I were in your place, I'd have no qualms about marrying the governor and making Captain Candide's fortune."

While the old woman was speaking with all the prudence that comes with age and experience, a little ship was seen entering the harbor. On board it were a magistrate and a number of police officers; here is what had happened:

The old woman had been quite right in suspecting that it was a Conventual Franciscan who had stolen Cunegonde's money and jewels in the town of Badajoz, when she and Candide were fleeing together. The monk tried to sell some of the precious stones to a jeweler. The merchant recognized them as belonging to the Grand Inquisitor. Before being hanged, the Franciscan confessed to having stolen them. He described the people he had robbed and the direction in which they were headed. It was already known that Cunegonde and Candide had fled. They were traced to Cadiz. A ship was sent in pursuit of them without delay. This ship was now in the harbor of Buenos Aires. The rumor spread that the magistrate was going to come ashore, and that he and his men were pursuing the murderers of the Grand Inquisitor. The prudent old woman instantly saw what had to be done. "You can't flee," she said to Cunegonde, "and you have nothing to fear: you're not the one who killed the Inquisitor. Besides, the governor loves you and won't let anyone mistreat you. Stay here." She then hurried to Candide and said to him, "Flee, or within an hour you'll be burned!"

There was not one moment to lose—but how could he part from Cunegonde, and where could he take refuge?

CHAPTER XIV

How Candide and Cacambo were received by the Jesuits of Paraguay.

CANDIDE had brought with him from Cadiz a valet of a type often found on the coasts of Spain and in the colonies. He was a quarter Spanish, born of a half-Indian father in the Tucumán province of Argentina. He had been a choir boy, a sexton, a sailor, a monk, a commercial agent, a soldier and a servant. His name was Cacambo, and he loved his master because his master was a very good man. He quickly saddled the two Andalusian horses and said, "Come, sir, let's follow the old woman's advice: let's ride away without looking back."

Candide shed tears. "Oh, my darling Cunegonde!" he said. "Must I leave you just when the governor is about to celebrate our wedding? I've brought you so far from home, Cunegonde: what will become of you now?"

"She'll become whatever she can," said Cacambo. "Women always manage to find something to do with themselves; God looks after them. Let's go."

"Where are you taking me?" asked Candide. "Where are we going? What will we do without Cunegonde?"

"By Saint James of Compostella," said Cacambo, "you were going to fight against the Jesuits: let's go and fight for them! I know the roads; I'll take you to their kingdom, and they'll be glad to have a captain who knows the Bulgar drills. You'll make a tremendous fortune. If a man doesn't get what he wants in one world, he can find it in another. It's always a great pleasure to see and do new things."

"So you've been in Paraguay before?" asked Candide.

"I certainly have," said Cacambo. "I was once a servant in the College of the Assumption, and I know the Fathers' government as well as I know the streets of Cadiz. Their government is a wonderful thing. The kingdom is already more than seven hundred fifty miles across, and it's divided into thirty provinces. The Fathers have everything, the people nothing; it's a masterpiece of reason and justice. I don't know of anyone as divine as the Fathers: over here, they wage war against the King of Spain and the King of Portugal, and in Europe they're the confessors of those same kings; here they kill Spaniards, in Madrid they send them to heaven. I find the whole thing delightful. Come with me, you're going to be the happiest man in the world. How glad the Fathers will be when they learn that a captain who knows the Bulgar drills has come to them!"

As soon as they reached the first border post, Cacambo told the guard that a captain wished to speak to the commandant. Word was sent to headquarters. A Paraguayan officer hurried to the feet of the commandant to tell him the news. Candide and Cacambo were first of all disarmed, and their Andalusian horses were taken from them. The two strangers were brought in between two ranks of soldiers, at the end of which was the commandant, with a three-cornered hat on his head, his robe tucked up, a sword at his side and a pike in his hand. He made a sign and the two newcomers were instantly surrounded by twenty-four soldiers. A sergeant told them they would have to wait, that the commandant could not speak to them, and that the Reverend Father Provincial did not allow any Spaniard to open his mouth in his presence or remain in the country for more than three hours.

"Where is the Reverend Father Provincial?" asked Cacambo.

"He's gone to the parade ground, after saying his mass," replied the sergeant, "and you won't be able to kiss his spurs for another three hours."

"But," said Cacambo, "my captain and I are starving, and he's not a Spaniard: he's a German. Couldn't

53

we have something to eat while we're waiting for His Reverence?"

The sergeant went straight to the commandant and reported this conversation to him.

"God be praised!" said the commandant. "Since he's a German, I can talk to him. Have him brought to my arbor."

Candide was immediately shown into a shady retreat adorned with a pretty colonnade of green and gold marble, and trelliswork cages enclosing parrots, colibris, hummingbirds, guinea fowl and all sorts of other rare birds. An excellent meal had been served in golden vessels, and while the Paraguayans were eating corn from wooden bowls in the blazing sunlight of the open fields, His Reverence the Commandant entered his arbor.

He was a handsome young man with a round face, a fair complexion, red cheeks, arched eyebrows, bright eyes, pink ears and crimson lips; he had an air of pride, but it was not the pride of a Spaniard or a Jesuit. Candide and Cacambo were given back their weapons and their Andalusian horses, which had been taken away from them. Cacambo fed them their oats near the arbor and kept an eye on them, for fear of a surprise.

After Candide had kissed the hem of the commandant's robe, they sat down to table.

"So you're a German?" said the Jesuit in that language.

"Yes, Reverend Father," said Candide.

As they spoke these words, they looked at each other in amazement, and with uncontrollable emotion.

"And what part of Germany are you from?" asked the Jesuit.

"From the dirty province of Westphalia," said Candide. "I was born in the castle of Thunder-ten-tronckh."

"O heaven!" exclaimed the commandant. "Is it possible?"

"What a miracle!" exclaimed Candide.

"Is it really you?" said the commandant.

"It can't be possible!" said Candide.

They both fell back in astonishment, then they embraced each other and shed torrents of tears.

"What! Is it really you, Reverend Father? You, the brother of my fair Cunegonde! You who were killed by the Bulgars! You, the son of My Lord the Baron! You, a Jesuit in Paraguay! This world is a strange place, there's no denying it! Oh, Pangloss, Pangloss! How happy you'd be if you hadn't been hanged!"

The commandant dismissed the Negro slaves and Paraguayans who were serving wine to them in rock-crystal goblets. He gave a thousand thanks to God and Saint Ignatius and clasped Candide in his arms while tears flowed down their cheeks.

"You'll be still more amazed, more deeply moved and more excited," said Candide, "when I tell you that your sister, Lady Cunegonde, whom you thought to have been disemboweled, is in the best of health."

"Where is she?"

"Not far from here: in Buenos Aires, with the governor. I'd come to make war on you."

Each word they spoke during their long conversation brought some new wonder to light. Their whole souls flew from their tongues, listened attentively in their ears, sparkled in their eyes. Since they were Germans, they sat at table for a long time, awaiting the Reverend Father Provincial, and the commandant spoke to his dear Candide as follows.

CHAPTER XV

How Candide killed the brother of his beloved Cunegonde.

ALL my life I'll remember the horrible day when I saw my parents killed and my sister raped. When the Bulgars had gone, my adorable sister couldn't be found. My parents and I were put in a cart, along with the bodies of two maidservants and three little boys who'd been murdered, and taken away to be buried in a Jesuit chapel five miles from our ancestral castle. A Jesuit sprinkled holy water on us. It was terribly salty, and a few drops of it got into my eyes. The Jesuit saw my eyelids flutter; he put his hand over my heart and felt it beating. I was given the care I needed, and three months later I was as good as new. As you know, my dear Candide, I was very handsome; I became even handsomer, so the Reverend Father Croust, the abbot of the house, took a great liking to me, and some time later I was sent to Rome. The Father General needed a group of young German Jesuit recruits. The rulers of Paraguay take in as few Spanish Jesuits as they can. They prefer foreigners because they feel they can control them better. The Reverend Father General decided I was fit to go and work in this vineyard. I left with a Pole and a Tyrolean. When I arrived I was given the honor of being made a subdeacon and a lieutenant. Today I'm a colonel and a priest. We'll give a hot reception to the King of Spain's troops: I guarantee you they'll be excommunicated and beaten. Providence has sent you here to help us. But is it true that my dear sister Cunegonde is near here, with the Governor of Buenos Aires?"

Candide swore to him that nothing could be truer. Their tears began to flow again.

The baron never tired of embracing Candide, and he called him his brother and savior. "Ah, my dear Candide," he said, "perhaps we can enter the city together as victors and rescue my sister Cunegonde."

"I hope so," said Candide, "because I intended to marry her, and I still do."

"You insolent wretch!" answered the baron. "How impudent of you even to think of marrying my sister, who has seventy-two generations of nobility behind her! You ought to be ashamed of yourself for daring to mention such an audacious scheme to me!"

Candide, petrified on hearing this, replied to him, "Reverend Father, all the generations of nobility in the world would make no difference. I rescued your sister from the arms of a Jew and an Inquisitor; she's under great obligation to me, and she wants to marry me. Dr. Pangloss always told me that all men are equal, and I will certainly marry her."

"We'll see tbout that, you scoundrel!" said the Jesuit Baron Thunder-ten-tronckh, and at the same time he struck him across the face with the flat of his sword. Candide instantly drew his own sword and plunged it to the hilt in the Jesuit baron's belly; but when he drew it out he began to weep.

"Dear God!" he said. "I've killed my former master, my friend, my brother-in-law! I'm the kindest man in the world, yet I've already killed three men, and two of them were priests!"

Cacambo, who had been standing watch at the entrance of the arbor, came running in. "There's nothing left for us to do except sell our lives dearly," his master said to him. "They'll surely come into the arbor—we must die sword in hand."

Cacambo, having been in tight spots before, did not lose his head. He took the baron's Jesuit robe, put it on Candide, gave him the dead man's hat and made him mount his horse. All this was done in the twinkling of an eye.

"Now let's gallop away, sir!" he said. "Everyone will take you for a Jesuit carrying orders, and we'll cross the border before they can come after us."

With these words he dashed forward, shouting in Spanish, "Make way, make way for the Reverend Father Colonel!"

CHAPTER XVI

What happened to the two travelers with two girls, two monkeys, and the savages known as the Oreillons.

CANDIDE and his valet had passed the border guards before anyone in the camp knew of the German Jesuit's death. The vigilant Cacambo had been careful

to fill his saddlebag with bread, chocolate, ham, fruit and a few bottles of wine. On their Andalusian horses, they plunged into unknown country where they found no road. Finally they came to a beautiful meadow intersected by streams. Our two travelers let their horses graze. Cacambo suggested to his master that they should eat, and he set him an example.

"How do you expect me to eat ham," said Candide, "when I've just killed the baron's son, and find myself doomed never to see the fair Cunegonde again for the rest of my life? What's the use of prolonging my miserable days, since I must drag them out far away from her, in remorse and despair? And what will the *Journal de Trévoux*[5] say?"

As he spoke thus, he continued to eat. The sun was setting. The two lost travelers heard little cries which seemed to come from women. They did not know whether they were cries of pain or of joy, but they leapt to their feet with the anxiety and alarm which everything arouses in an unknown country. The cries came from two naked girls who were running nimbly along the edge of the meadow while two monkeys followed them, biting their buttocks. Candide was moved to pity. He had learned to shoot in the Bulgar army, and he could have shot a hazelnut from a tree without touching the leaves. He picked up his double-barreled Spanish rifle and fired, killing the two monkeys.

"God be praised, my dear Cacambo: I've delivered those two poor creatures from a great danger! If I sinned in killing an Inquisitor and a Jesuit, I've atoned for it by saving the lives of two girls. They may be young ladies of noble birth, and the incident may bring us great advantages in this country."

He was about to go on, but his tongue suddenly became paralyzed when he saw the girls lovingly embrace the monkeys, burst into tears over their bodies and fill the air with grief-stricken cries.

"I wasn't expecting such tender compassion," he said at length to Cacambo.

"That was a fine thing to do, sir!" said Cacambo. "You've killed those young ladies' lovers!"

"Their lovers? Impossible! You're joking, Cacambo! How could I believe such a thing?"

"My dear master," replied Cacambo, "you're always surprised by everything. Why do you find it so strange that in some countries there should be monkeys that enjoy the favors of ladies? They're a quarter human, just as I'm a quarter Spanish."

"Alas," said Candide, "I do remember hearing Dr. Pangloss say that similar incidents had happened in the past, that such mixtures had produced Aegipans, fauns and satyrs, and that several great men of antiquity had seen them; but I regarded all that as fables."

"Now you should be convinced that it's true," said Cacambo, "and you can see how people behave when they've been given a different upbringing. All I'm afraid of is that those ladies may make trouble for us."

These well-founded reflections determined Candide to leave the meadow and go into the forest. He and Cacambo ate supper there, and, after cursing the Inquisitor of Portugal, the Governor of Buenos Aires and the baron, they both went to sleep on the moss. When they awoke they found that they could not move. The reason for this was that during the night the Oreillons, the inhabitants of the country, to whom the two ladies had denounced them, had tied them up with ropes made of bark. They were surrounded by about fifty naked Oreillons armed with arrows, clubs and stone axes. Some of them were heating a large cauldron of water, others were preparing spits, and all were shouting, "He's a Jesuit, he's a Jesuit! We'll have our revenge, and eat a good meal! Let's eat Jesuit, let's eat Jesuit!"

"I was right, dear master," cried Cacambo sadly, "when I told you those two girls would make trouble for us!"

Seeing the cauldron and the spits, Candide cried out, "We're surely going to be either roasted or boiled. Ah, what would Dr. Pangloss say if he saw what pure nature is like? All is well, I won't argue about it; but

I must admit it's a cruel fate to have lost Lady Cunegonde and then be roasted on a spit by the Oreillons."

Cacambo never lost his head. "Don't give up hope," he said to the forlorn Candide. "I know a little of these people's jargon, and I'm going to speak to them."

"Be sure to point out to them how horribly inhuman it is to cook men," said Candide, "and how unchristian it is, too."

"Gentlemen," said Cacambo, "you expect to eat a Jesuit today; that's perfectly all right: nothing could be more just than to treat your enemies that way, for natural law teaches us to kill our neighbor, and that's how people behave all over the world. If we don't exercise the right to eat him, it's because we have other things to make a good meal of. But you don't have the same resources as we do, and it's certainly better to eat your enemies than abandon the fruit of your victory to crows and ravens. However, gentlemen, you wouldn't want to eat your friends. You think you're about to put a Jesuit on the spit, but you're actually about to roast your defender, the enemy of your enemies. I myself was born in your country, and this gentleman is my master. Far from being a Jesuit, he's just killed a Jesuit and is wearing his clothes: that's the cause of your mistake. To verify what I'm saying, take his robe, bring it to the nearest border post of the Fathers' kingdom, and find out whether or not my master has killed a Jesuit officer. It won't take long, and you can still eat us if you find out I've lied to you. But if I've told the truth, you're too well acquainted with the principles of international law, morality and justice not to spare our lives."

The Oreillons found this speech quite reasonable. They appointed two notables to inquire into the truth of the matter. The two delegates carried out their mission intelligently and soon returned with good news. The Oreillons untied their prisoners, treated them with great courtesy, offered them women, gave them refreshments and led them to the border of their territory, shouting joyfully: "He's not a Jesuit, he's not a Jesuit!"

Candide was filled with wonder at the cause of his deliverance. "What a people!" he kept exclaiming. "What men! What morality! If I hadn't been lucky enough to thrust my sword through the body of Lady Cunegonde's brother, I'd surely have been eaten. But pure nature is good after all, since, instead of eating me, these people showered me with polite kindness as soon as they found out I wasn't a Jesuit."

CHAPTER XVII

How Candide and his valet came to the land of Eldorado.

WHEN they reached the border of the Oreillons' territory, Cacambo said to Candide, "You see: this hemisphere is no better than the other one; believe me, the best thing we can do is go back to Europe by the shortest route possible."

"How can we?" said Candide. "And where could I go? If I go back to my country, I'll find the Bulgars and the Avars slaughtering everyone in sight; if I return to Portugal, I'll be burned; if we stay here, we're in constant danger of being put on a spit. But how can I bring myself to leave the part of the world Lady Cunegonde is living in?"

"Let's head for Cayenne," said Cacambo. "We'll find some Frenchmen there who travel all over the world, and they'll be able to help us. Perhaps God will take pity on us."

It was not easy to get to Cayenne; they knew approximately what direction to take, but there were terrible obstacles everywhere: mountains, rivers, precipices, bandits and savages. Their horses died of fatigue, and they used up all their provisions. After eating nothing but wild fruits for a whole month, they came at last to a stream whose banks were lined with coconut trees which sustained their lives and their hopes.

Cacambo, whose advice was always as good as the old woman's, said to Candide, "We can't go on like this, we've walked enough. I see an empty boat on the bank: let's fill it with coconuts, get into it and drift with the current—a river always leads to some inhabited spot. If we don't find anything pleasant, we'll at least find something new."

"Let's go," said Candide. "We'll place ourselves in the hands of Providence."

They drifted for several miles between banks that were sometimes covered with flowers, sometimes arid, sometimes flat, and sometimes steep. The river grew steadily wider, until at last it vanished into a vault of awe-inspiring rocks that rose up to the sky. The two travelers had the courage to abandon themselves to the stream as it flowed under this vault. The river narrowed at this spot and bore them along with terrible speed and noise. After twenty-four hours they saw daylight again, but their boat was smashed against a reef. They had to crawl from rock to rock for nearly three miles, until finally they saw a vast horizon bordered by unscalable mountains. The land here was cultivated for pleasure as well as from necessity; everywhere the useful had been made pleasant. The roads were covered, or rather adorned, with beautifully formed carriages made of lustrous material, carrying men and women of extraordinary beauty and swiftly drawn by large red sheep whose speed surpassed that of the finest horses of Andalusia, Tetuán or Meknes.

"Here's a better country than Westphalia!" said Candide.

He and Cacambo entered the first village they came to. Several children, wearing tattered gold brocade, were playing quoits at the edge of this village. Our two men from the other world stopped to watch them. Their quoits were rather large round objects, yellow, red or green, which shone with extraordinary brilliance. Our travelers picked up a few of them and found that some were made of gold, while others were emeralds or rubies; the smallest one of them would have been the greatest ornament of a Mogul's throne.

"These children playing quoits," said Cacambo, "must be the sons of the king of this country."

Just then the village schoolmaster came out to call the children back to school.

"There's the tutor of the royal family," said Candide.

The little urchins immediately stopped playing, leaving their quoits and other playthings on the ground. Candide picked them up, ran to the tutor and humbly presented them to him, making signs to point out to him that Their Royal Highnesses had forgotten their gold and jewels. The village schoolmaster smiled, dropped them on the ground, looked at Candide for a moment in great surprise, then turned and went on his way.

The travelers did not fail to pick up the gold, rubies and emeralds.

"Where are we?" cried Candide. "The children of the kings of this country must be well brought up, since they're taught to despise gold and jewels."

Cacambo was as surprised as Candide. Finally they came to the first house of the village. It was built like a European palace. Large numbers of people were crowding around the door, and there were even more inside. They could hear delightful music, and smell a delicious odor of cooking. Cacambo walked up to the door and heard that the people were speaking Peruvian, his native tongue, for, as everyone knows, Cacambo was born in Tucumán, in a village where that was the only language known.

"I'll be your interpreter," he said to Candide. "Let's go inside: this is an inn."

Two waiters and two waitresses, dressed in gold cloth, with their hair tied in ribbons, immediately invited them to sit down to table. They were served four tureens of soup, each garnished with two parrots, a boiled condor weighing two hundred pounds, two roasted monkeys of excellent flavor, three hundred colibris in one dish and six hundred hummingbirds

64

in another; there were also exquisite stews and delicious pastries, and everything was served in dishes made of a kind of rock crystal. The waiters and waitresses poured out various liqueurs made from sugar cane.

The other guests were mostly merchants and carters, all extremely polite. They asked Cacambo a few questions with the most delicate discretion, and gave satisfactory answers to the questions he asked them.

When the meal was over, Cacambo and Candide thought they had amply paid their bill when they left on the table two of the big pieces of gold they had picked up, but the host and hostess burst out laughing and held their sides for a long time.

"Gentlemen," said the host, "it's easy to see you're not from our country, and we're not used to foreigners. Excuse us for laughing when you offered to pay us with two stones from our roads. You probably have none of our money, but you don't need any to dine here. All inns run for the convenience of people engaged in commerce are paid for by the government. You've fared badly here, because this is a poor village, but everywhere else you'll be given the reception you deserve."

Cacambo explained the host's remarks to Candide, who listened to them with the same wonder and bewilderment his friend felt as he translated them.

"What country can this be," said one to the other, "unknown to the rest of the world and so different in every way from anything we've ever seen before? It's probably the country where everything goes well, because there must be one like that somewhere. And, despite what Dr. Pangloss used to say, I often noticed that everything went rather badly in Westphalia."

CHAPTER XVIII

What they saw in the land of Eldorado.

CACAMBO expressed his extreme curiosity to the host, who said to him, "I'm very ignorant, and quite happy to stay that way, but we have here an old man who's retired from the court: he's the most learned man in the kingdom, and the most communicative."

He immediately took Cacambo to the old man's house. Candide, relegated to a secondary role, accompanied his valet. The house they entered was a very simple one, for its door was made only of silver, and the rooms were paneled only with gold, although the workmanship was in such good taste that the richest paneling was not superior. The antechamber was incrusted only with rubies and emeralds, it is true, but the order in which everything was arranged made up for this extreme simplicity.

The old man received the two strangers sitting on a sofa stuffed with colibri feathers and had them served liqueurs in diamond goblets. He then satisfied their curiosity as follows:

"I'm a hundred seventy-two years old, and my father, the king's equerry, told me about the amazing Peruvian revolutions he witnessed. This kingdom is the former land of the Incas, who rashly left it to go off and subjugate another part of the world, and who were finally destroyed by the Spaniards.

"The princes of their royal family who remained in their native land showed greater wisdom: with the consent of the nation, they ordained that no inhabitant of our little kingdom should ever leave it, and that's what has preserved our innocence and our happiness. The Spaniards had a confused knowledge of this country, which they called Eldorado, and an Englishman named Raleigh came quite close to it about a hundred years ago. But since we're surrounded by unscalable mountains and cliffs, so far we've been safe from the rapacity of European nations, who have an incredible lust for the pebbles and dirt of our land, and would kill every one of us to get them."

The conversation was long; it touched on the form of government, customs and morals, women, public spectacles and the arts. Finally Candide, who was always interested in metaphysics, told Cacambo to ask whether the country had a religion.

The old man blushed slightly. "What!" he exclaimed. "Can you doubt that we have a religion? Do you think we're ingrates?"

Cacambo humbly asked him what the religion of Eldorado was. The old man blushed again and said, "Can there be two religions? We have, I believe, the same religion as everyone else: we worship God, morning and night."

"Do you worship only one God?" asked Cacambo, still serving as the interpreter of Candide's doubts.

"Of course!" said the old man. "There aren't two Gods, or three, or four. I must say that people from your world ask very strange questions!"

Candide continued to press the kindly old man with questions. He wanted to know how people prayed in Eldorado.

"We don't pray," said the venerable sage. "We have nothing to ask of God: He's given us everything we need. We constantly thank him."

Candide was curious to see some of their priests; he asked where they were. The kindly old man smiled and said, "My friends, we're all priests. The king and all heads of families solemnly sing hymns of thanksgiving every morning, accompanied by an orchestra of five or six thousand musicians."

"What! You have no monks who teach, argue, rule, plot, and burn people who don't agree with them?"

"We'd be mad if we did," said the old man. "We all agree with each other here, and we don't know what you mean when you talk about your monks."

Candide was enraptured as he listened to all this, and he said to himself, "This is quite different from

Westphalia and the baron's castle. If our friend Pangloss had seen Eldorado, he wouldn't have said that the castle of Thunder-ten-tronckh was the finest thing on earth. It's obvious that everyone ought to travel."

After this long conversation, the kindly old man had six sheep harnessed to a carriage and assigned twelve of his servants to take the two travelers to court.

"Forgive me," he said to them, "for not accompanying you: my age deprives me of that honor. The king will give you a reception with which you won't be dissatisfied, and I'm sure you'll excuse the customs of our country if some of them displease you."

Candide and Cacambo got into the carriage, the six sheep set off at great speed, and in less than four hours they reached the king's palace, which stood at one end of the capital. Its portal was two hundred twenty feet high and a hundred feet wide. It would be impossible to describe the material it was made of, but it is easy to understand how enormously superior it must have been to the pebbles and sand we call precious stones and gold.

When Candide and Cacambo alighted from the carriage, they were received by twenty beautiful girls attached to the palace; they took the visitors to the baths and dressed them in robes made of hummingbird down. The great lords and ladies of the court then led them to His Majesty's apartments, passing between two ranks of a thousand musicians each, according to custom. As they were approaching the throne room, Cacambo asked a great lord how they should behave when they were brought into His Majesty's presence: whether they should fall to their knees or flat on their faces, whether they should put their hands on their heads or on their behinds, whether they should lick the dust on the floor—in short, what the proper procedure was.

"The custom," said the lord, "is to embrace the king and kiss him on both cheeks."

Candide and Cacambo threw their arms around His Majesty's neck; he gave them an extremely gracious welcome and courteously invited them to supper.

In the meantime, they were shown around the city; they saw public buildings that rose up to the clouds, market places adorned with countless columns, fountains of clear water, pink water or sugar-cane liqueurs which flowed continuously in broad public squares paved with a kind of precious stone that gave off an odor like that of cloves and cinnamon. Candide asked to see the law courts; he was told that there were none, that lawsuits were unknown. He asked if there were prisons; the answer was no. What surprised and delighted him most of all was the Palace of Science, where he saw a gallery two thousand paces long filled with instruments of mathematics and physics.

After they had spent the whole afternoon covering about a thousandth of the city, they were taken back to the royal palace. Candide sat down to table with His Majesty, his valet Cacambo and several ladies. No better meal was ever served, and no supper conversation was ever more sparkling than His Majesty's. Cacambo explained his witty remarks to Candide, and they seemed witty even in translation. Of all the things that amazed Candide, this was by no means the least amazing.

They spent a month in the palace. Candide kept saying to Cacambo, "Once again, my friend, I admit that there's no comparison between this country and the castle where I was born; but it's still true that Lady Cunegonde isn't here, and you must have some mistress in Europe too. If we stay here, we'll only be like everyone else, but if we go back to our world with no more than twelve sheep laden with stones from Eldorado, we'll be richer than all the kings of Europe put together, we'll have no more Inquisitors to fear, and we can easily rescue Lady Cunegonde."

Cacambo was pleased to hear this; a man who has traveled always enjoys coming home to show off and tell impressive stories about the things he has seen abroad. So the two fortunate men decided to be fortunate no longer: they asked His Majesty for permission to leave.

"It's a foolish thing to do," said the king. "I know

my country doesn't amount to much, but when a man is fairly well off somewhere, he ought to stay there. I certainly have no right to prevent foreigners from leaving: that kind of tyranny is sanctioned by neither our customs nor our laws. All men are free. You may leave whenever you like, but you'll have a very difficult journey. It's impossible to sail against the current of the river that miraculously brought you here, and which flows through vaults of rock. The mountains surrounding my kingdom are ten thousand feet high and as steep as a wall; they're all over twenty-five miles wide, and they drop straight down on the other side. However, since you're determined to leave, I'll order my mechanical engineers to construct a machine that will carry you in comfort. When you've been taken over the mountains, no one can go with you any further, because my subjects have all sworn never to go beyond them, and they're too wise to break their word. But you may ask me for anything else you wish."

"All we ask of Your Majesty," said Cacambo, "is a few sheep laden with food and some of the pebbles and mud of your country."

The king laughed and said, "I can't understand why you people from Europe are so fond of our yellow mud, but take as much as you like, you're welcome to it."

He immediately ordered his engineers to make a machine to hoist the two extraordinary men out of the kingdom. Three thousand learned scientists worked on it; it was finished in two weeks and cost no more than twenty thousand pounds sterling in the currency of the country. Candide and Cacambo were placed on the machine. There were two large red sheep, saddled and bridled, for them to ride after they had crossed the mountains, twenty pack-sheep laden with food, thirty bearing gifts consisting of some of the country's most remarkable products, and fifty laden with gold, diamonds and other precious stones. The king affectionately embraced the two wanderers.

Their departure was a wonderful sight, and so was the ingenious way in which they and their sheep were lifted over the mountains. The scientists took leave of them after placing them in safety. Candide had no other desire and aim than to go and present his sheep to Lady Cunegonde.

"We now have enough to pay the Governor of Buenos Aires," he said, "if Lady Cunegonde's freedom can be bought. Let's go to Cayenne and set sail from there, then we'll see what kingdom we can buy."

CHAPTER XIX

What happened to them at Surinam, and how Candide became acquainted with Martin.

THE first day of their journey was rather pleasant. They were heartened by the thought that they now possessed more treasure than all of Asia, Europe and Africa could assemble. Candide, elated, wrote Cunegonde's name on the trees. On the second day, two of their sheep sank in a bog and were swallowed up with their loads; two more sheep died of fatigue a few days later; then seven or eight of them perished from hunger in a desert; still others fell off cliffs. Finally, after they had traveled for a hundred days, only two sheep were left. Candide said to Cacambo, "Now you see, my friend, how perishable are the riches of this world. There's nothing solid but virtue, and the happiness of seeing Lady Cunegonde again."

"I agree," said Cacambo, "but we still have two sheep carrying more treasure than the King of Spain will ever have, and in the distance I see a town which I surmise to be Surinam, a Dutch possession. Our troubles are over, our happiness is about to begin."

As they were approaching the town they saw a Negro lying on the ground. His only garment was a pair of short blue trousers, and they had been half torn away. The poor man's left leg and right hand were missing.

"Good heavens!" Candide said to him in Dutch. "What are you doing here in such a terrible state?"

"I'm waiting for my master, Mynheer Vanderdendur the famous merchant," replied the Negro.

"Was it Mynheer Vanderdendur who put you in that condition?" asked Candide.

"Yes, sir," said the Negro, "it's the custom. We're given a pair of short trousers twice a year as our only clothing. If we get a finger caught under the millstone while we're working in the sugar mills, they cut off the whole hand; and if we try to run away, they cut off one of our legs. I've been in both those situations. That's the price of the sugar you eat in Europe. However when my mother sold me on the Guinea coast for ten patagons, she said to me, 'My dear child, always glorify and worship our fetishes, they'll make you live happily. You now have the honor of being a slave of our lords the white men, and in acquiring that honor you've made your parents' fortune.' I may have made their fortune, but they didn't make mine. Dogs, monkeys and parrots are a thousand times less miserable than we are. The Dutch fetishes, who converted me, tell me every Sunday that we're all children of Adam, black and white alike. I'm no genealogist, but if those preachers are telling the truth, we're all cousins, and you must admit that no one could treat his relatives more horribly."

"Oh, Pangloss!" cried Candide. "This is an abomination you never dreamed of! It's too much: I'll have to give up your optimism at last."

"What's optimism?" asked Cacambo.

"Alas," said Candide, "it's a mania for insisting that everything is all right when everything is going wrong."

He wept as he looked at the Negro, and there were still tears in his eyes when he entered Surinam.

The first thing they asked was whether there was any ship in the harbor that could be sent to Buenos Aires. The man they spoke to happened to be a Spanish captain. He offered to strike an honest bargain with them, and told them to meet him later at an inn. Candide and the faithful Cacambo went there with their two sheep to wait for him.

Candide, who never concealed what was in his heart, related all his adventures to the Spaniard and admitted that he wanted to rescue Lady Cunegonde.

"Then I certainly won't take you to Buenos Aires," said the captain. "I'd be hanged, and so would you. The fair Cunegonde is the governor's favorite mistress."

This was a terrible blow to Candide, and he wept for a long time. Finally he drew Cacambo aside and said to him, "Here's what you must do, my dear friend. We each have diamonds worth five or six million in our pockets. You're more resourceful than I am: go to Buenos Aires and get Lady Cunegonde. If the governor makes any difficulties, give him a million; if he still refuses, give him two million. You've never killed an Inquisitor, so they won't mistrust you. I'll fit out another ship and go to Venice to wait for you. Venice is a free state where there's nothing to fear from Bulgars, Avars, Jews or Inquisitors."

Cacambo praised this wise plan. He was in despair at having to be separated from a good master who had become his close friend, but the pleasure of being useful to him overcame the sorrow of leaving him. They embraced each other with tears in their eyes. Candide urged him not to forget the good old woman. Cacambo left the same day. A fine man, that Cacambo!

Candide stayed on a while longer in Surinam, waiting for another captain to take him to Italy with the two sheep he had left. He hired servants and bought everything he would need for a long voyage. Finally Mynheer Vanderdendur, the master of a large ship, came to him and introduced himself.

"How much would you charge," Candide asked him, "to take me straight to Venice, along with my servants, my baggage and these two sheep?"

The captain asked for ten thousand piasters. Candide agreed without hesitation.

"Aha!" thought the prudent Vanderdendur. "This foreigner is ready to give ten thousand piasters all at once! He must be very rich." He came back a short time later and announced that he could not sail for less than twenty thousand.

"All right, then," said Candide, "you'll have twenty thousand."

"Good heavens!" the captain said to himself. "This man gives twenty thousand piasters as easily as ten thousand!" He came back again and said he could not take him to Venice for less than thirty thousand piasters.

"Then you'll have thirty thousand," replied Candide.

"Aha!" the Dutch captain said to himself again. "Thirty thousand piasters mean nothing to this man. His two sheep must be laden with immense treasures. I won't press him any further; first I'll make him pay the thirty thousand, then we'll see."

Candide sold two little diamonds, the smaller of which was worth more than all the money the captain asked. He paid him in advance. The two sheep were put on board. Candide followed in a small boat to join the ship in the harbor. The captain seized his opportunity: he set his sails and weighed anchor. The wind favored him. Candide, frantic and bewildered, soon lost sight of him. "Alas!" he cried. "That's a trick worthy of the Old World!" He turned back to shore, overwhelmed with sorrow, for he had lost enough to make the fortune of twenty monarchs.

He went to see the Dutch judge, and since he was rather agitated he pounded loudly on the door. He went in, explained what had happened and shouted a little more loudly than was proper. The judge began by fining him ten thousand piasters for the noise he had made. Then he listened patiently, promised to investigate his case as soon as the captain returned, and charged him another ten thousand piasters for the expenses of the hearing.

This behavior was the last straw: it drove Candide to despair. He had experienced misfortunes that were actually a thousand times more painful, but the cold-bloodedness of the judge, and of the captain who had robbed him, inflamed his resentment and plunged him into black melancholy. The wickedness of men appeared to him in all its ugliness, and his mind was filled with gloomy thoughts. Finally he found a French ship ready to leave for Bordeaux. Since he had no more sheep laden with diamonds to take on board, he rented a cabin on the ship for a fair price and had it announced in the town that he would give passage, food and two thousand piasters to an honest man willing to make the voyage with him, provided he was the most unfortunate man in the province, and the one most disgusted with his situation.

Applicants came to him in such great numbers that a whole fleet of ships could not have held them all. Candide, wishing to make his choice from among the most likely-looking ones, picked out about twenty who appeared to be rather sociable, and who all claimed to deserve his preference. He assembled them at his inn and gave them supper on condition that each one of them swear to relate his story faithfully. He told them he would choose the one who seemed to be the most deserving of pity and to have the best reasons for being dissatisfied with his lot, and he promised to give the others a small gratification.

The session lasted till four in the morning. As he listened to all their adventures, Candide recalled what the old woman had told him on the way to Buenos Aires, and how she had wagered that there was no one on the ship who had not suffered grave misfortunes. He thought of Pangloss with each story he heard. "That Pangloss," he said to himself, "would have a hard time defending his system. I wish he were here. If all goes well, it's in Eldorado, not in the rest of the world." He finally decided in favor of a poor scholar who had spent ten years working for the Amsterdam publishers. He judged that there was no profession on earth with which a man could be more thoroughly disgusted.

Furthermore, this scholar, who was a good man, had been robbed by his wife, beaten by his son and abandoned by his daughter, who had eloped with a Portuguese. He had just lost the minor post that had been his only means of support, and he was persecuted by the preachers of Surinam because they believed him to be a Socinian.[6] It must be admitted that the others were at least equally unfortunate, but Candide hoped that the scholar would help him while away the time during his voyage. His rivals all felt that Candide had done them a great injustice, but he appeased them by giving each of them a hundred piasters.

CHAPTER XX

What happened to Candide and Martin at sea.

AND so the old scholar, whose name was Martin, set out for Bordeaux with Candide. They had both seen and suffered much; if the ship had been sailing for Japan by way of the Cape of Good Hope, they would have been able to discuss moral and physical evil during the entire voyage.

Candide had one great advantage over Martin, however: he still hoped to see Lady Cunegonde again, while Martin had nothing to hope for. Furthermore, Candide still had some gold and diamonds; and, although he had lost a hundred red sheep laden with the greatest treasures on earth, and although he was still incensed over the Dutch captain's treachery, when he thought about what he still had in his pockets, and when he spoke about Cunegonde, especially at the end of a meal, he still inclined toward Pangloss's doctrine.

"But tell me," he said to the scholar, "what do *you* think about all that? What are your views on moral and physical evil?"

"Sir," replied Martin, "my priests accused me of being a Socinian, but the truth of the matter is that I'm a Manichean."

"You're joking," said Candide, "there are no more Manicheans in the world."

"I'm one," said Martin. "I don't know what to do about it, but I can't think otherwise."

"You must be possessed by the devil," said Candide.

"He meddles so much in the affairs of this world," said Martin, "that he may well be inside me, and everywhere else too. But I confess that when I consider this globe, or rather this globule, I think that God has abandoned it to some malevolent being— with the exception of Eldorado. I've almost never seen a town that didn't desire the ruin of some neighboring town, or a family that didn't want to exterminate some other family. Everywhere in the world, the weak detest the strong and grovel before them, and the strong treat them like flocks of sheep to be sold for their meat and wool. A million regimented assassins sweep over Europe from one end to the other, murdering and robbing with discipline to earn their bread, because there's no more honorable occupation. And in towns that seem to enjoy peace, and where the arts flourish, the envies, cares and anxieties that assail the people are more numerous than the afflictions of a besieged town. Secret torments are even more agonizing than public miseries. In short, I've seen and experienced so much that I'm a Manichean."

"But there is *some* good in the world," replied Candide.

"Perhaps so," said Martin, "but I haven't seen it."

In the middle of this argument they heard a sound of gunfire which grew louder at every moment. Everyone took out his telescope and saw two ships fighting about three miles away. The wind brought them both so close to the French ship that those on board her had the pleasure of watching the fight in comfort. Finally one of the ships fired a broadside so low and so accurately that the other ship sank. Candide and Martin distinctly saw a hundred men on the deck of the sinking ship; they all raised their hands to heaven and uttered terrible cries; a moment later they had all been swallowed up by the sea.

"You see," said Martin, "that's how men treat each other."

"It's true that there was something diabolical in what we just saw," said Candide.

As he spoke, he saw something bright red in the water, moving toward his ship. A boat was lowered to find out what it might be. It was one of Candide's sheep. His joy at finding that sheep again was greater than his sorrow over losing a hundred of them, all laden with large diamonds from Eldorado.

The French captain soon learned that the captain of the victorious ship was a Spaniard, and that the captain of the sunken ship had been a Dutch pirate: the same man who had robbed Candide. The enormous wealth stolen by that scoundrel had gone to the bottom of the sea with him; only one sheep had been saved.

"This proves that crime is sometimes punished," Candide said to Martin. "That black-hearted Dutch captain has met the fate he deserved."

"Yes," said Martin, "but did all the passengers on his ship have to perish with him? God punished that scoundrel, but the devil drowned the others."

The French ship and the Spanish one continued on their way, and Candide continued his conversation with Martin. They argued steadily for two weeks, and at the end of that time they had gotten no further than they were at the beginning. But at least they had been talking, communicating ideas and consoling each other. Candide stroked his sheep. "Since I found you," he said, "I'm sure I can find Cunegonde again."

CHAPTER XXI

How Candide and Martin reasoned with each other as they approached the coast of France.

At last they sighted the coast of France.

"Have you ever been in France?" asked Candide.

"Yes," replied Martin, "I've traveled in several provinces. There are some where half the population is mad, others where the people are too crafty, others where they're generally rather gentle and rather stupid, others where they pride themselves on their wit; and in every province the chief occupations, in order of importance, are love-making, malicious gossip and talking nonsense."

"But haven't you ever been in Paris?"

"Yes, I've been in Paris: it's a mixture of everything found in all the provinces. It's a chaos, a restless throng in which everyone is looking for pleasure and hardly anyone ever finds it, or at least that's how it seemed to me. I stayed there for a while; as soon as I arrived, I was robbed of everything I had by pickpockets at the Saint-Germain fair. I was arrested as a thief myself, and I spent a week in jail. After that I worked for a printer as a proofreader, to earn enough for a trip back to Holland on foot. I became acquainted with the writing rabble, the scheming rabble and the fanatic rabble. I've heard there are very refined people in that city; I'm willing to be convinced."

"For my part, I have no curiosity to see France," said Candide. "You can easily understand that after spending a month in Eldorado, a man has no interest in seeing anything else on earth, except Lady Cunegonde. I'm going to wait for her in Venice. I'll cross France on the way to Italy—will you come with me?"

"I'll be glad to," said Martin. "I've been told that Venice is a good city only for Venetian noblemen, although foreigners are given a good reception if they're rich. You have money and I have none, so I'll go with you anywhere."

"By the way," said Candide, "do you think the earth was originally a sea, as it says in that big book that belongs to the captain of the ship?"

"I don't believe it at all," said Martin, "no more than I believe all the fantastic nonsense that's been written in the past few years."

"But for what purpose was the earth formed?" asked Candide.

"To drive us mad," replied Martin.

"Aren't you surprised by what I told you about those two Oreillon girls who were in love with two monkeys?" asked Candide.

"Not at all," said Martin. "I don't see anything odd about their passion. I've seen so many strange things that nothing is strange any more."

"Do you believe," said Candide, "that men have always slaughtered each other as they do today, that they've always been liars, cheats, traitors, ingrates and thieves, weak, fickle, cowardly, envious, greedy, drunken, miserly, ambitious, bloodthirsty, slanderous, lecherous, fanatical, hypocritical and foolish?"

"Do you believe," said Martin, "that hawks have always eaten pigeons when they find them?"

"Yes, of course," said Candide.

"Well, then," said Martin, "if hawks have always had the same character, what makes you think men may have changed theirs?"

"Oh!" said Candide. "There's a big difference, because free will . . ."

The discussion was still going on when they reached Bordeaux.

CHAPTER XXII

What happened to Candide and Martin in France.

CANDIDE stopped in Bordeaux only long enough to sell a few Eldorado pebbles and provide himself with a good carriage—a two-seated one, for he could no longer do without his philosopher, Martin. To his sorrow, however, he had to part with his sheep. He gave it to the Bordeaux Academy of Science, whose annual prize was awarded that year to the author of the best essay on the subject of why this sheep's wool was red. The winner was a scholar from the North who demonstrated by A plus B minus C divided by Z that the sheep had to be red and would die of sheeppox.

However, all the travelers Candide met at the inns along the road said to him, "We're going to Paris."

This general eagerness finally gave him a desire to see the French capital; it would not take him very far off the road to Venice.

He entered the city through the suburb of Saint-Marceau and thought he must be in the ugliest village in Westphalia.

Candide had scarcely put up at an inn when he was attacked by a slight illness caused by fatigue. Since he wore an enormous diamond on his finger, and since a prodigiously heavy strongbox had been noticed among his baggage, he was immediately surrounded by two doctors he had not sent for, several intimate friends who would not leave him, and two pious and charitable ladies who kept him supplied with hot broth.

"I remember being ill myself during my first stay in Paris," said Martin. "I was very poor, so I had no friends, altruistic ladies or doctors. I recovered."

With the aid of medicines and bloodlettings, Candide's illness became serious. A regular visitor of the neighborhood came to him and gently asked him for a note payable to the bearer in the next world.[7] Candide flatly refused. The pious ladies assured him it was the latest fashion. He replied that he was not a fashionable man. Martin wanted to throw the visitor out the window. The clergyman swore that Candide would not be buried. Martin swore that he would bury the clergyman if he continued to bother them. The quarrel became heated. Martin took him by the shoulders and roughly shoved him out of the room. This caused a great commotion, and a police report was made of the incident.

Candide recovered, and during his convalescence a number of distinguished people came to have supper with him. They gambled for high stakes. Candide was amazed that he never had any aces in his hand, but Martin was not surprised.

Among those who showed him around the city was a little abbé from Périgord, one of those assiduous, constantly alert and obliging, shameless, fawning and accommodating people who lie in wait for passing strangers, tell them all the scandalous gossip of the city and offer them pleasures at any price. First he took Candide and Martin to the theater, where a new tragedy was being presented. Candide was seated near several wits. This did not prevent him from weeping during perfectly performed scenes. During the intermission, one of the quibblers beside him said to him, "You're wrong to weep: that actress is very bad, the actor playing with her is worse still, and the play is even worse than the cast. The author doesn't know one word of Arabic, yet the scene is in Arabia. Furthermore, he's a man who doesn't believe in innate ideas. Tomorrow I'll bring you twenty pamphlets written against him."

"How many plays have been written in France?" Candide asked the abbé.

"Five or six thousand."

"That's a lot," said Candide. "How many of them are good?"

"Fifteen or sixteen," replied the abbé.

"That's a lot," said Martin.

Candide was greatly pleased by an actress who played the part of Queen Elizabeth in a rather dull tragedy that is sometimes performed. "That actress is very attractive," he said to Martin. "She bears a slight resemblance to Lady Cunegonde. I'd like to pay my respects to her."

The abbé offered to take him to her house. Candide, brought up in Germany, asked what the proper etiquette was, and how Queens of England were treated in France.

"That depends," replied the abbé. "In the provinces, they're taken to an inn; in Paris, they're respected when they're beautiful and thrown into the garbage dump when they're dead."

"Queens in the garbage dump?" exclaimed Candide.

"Yes, it's true," said Martin, "the abbé is right. I was in Paris when Mademoiselle Monime passed from this life to the next, to use a common expression. She was refused what these people call 'the honors of burial'; in other words, the honor of rotting with all the beggars of the neighborhood in some sordid cemetery. She was buried all by herself at a corner of the Rue de Bourgogne, which must have caused her great sorrow, because she had a noble mind."

"That was very impolite," said Candide.

"What can you expect?" asked Martin. "That's how these people are. Imagine every possible contradiction and inconsistency, and you will find them all in the government, law courts, churches and entertainments of this odd nation."

"Is it true that people in Paris are always laughing?" asked Candide.

"Yes," said the abbé, "but they're burning with rage at the same time. They complain about everything with gales of laughter, and they even laugh while they commit the most abominable crimes."

"Who's that fat pig," said Candide, "who was talking so vehemently against the play that made me weep so much, and against the actors who gave me so much pleasure?"

"He's a spiteful man," replied the abbé, "who earns his living by attacking all plays and all books. He hates anyone who succeeds, just as eunuchs hate anyone who makes love. He's one of those snakes of literature who feed on filth and venom; he's a hack."

"What do you mean by 'a hack'?" asked Candide.

"A man who writes for cheap rags, a F——8"

This conversation took place on the staircase, as Candide, Martin and the abbé watched the people streaming out of the theater after the performance.

"Although I'm very eager to see Lady Cunegonde again," said Candide, "I'd still like to have supper with Mademoiselle Clairon, because she made a deep impression on me."

The abbé was not the kind of man who could call on Mademoiselle Clairon: she received only distinguished company. "She's engaged this evening," he said, "but allow me the honor of taking you to visit a lady of quality in whose house you'll come to know Paris as though you'd been here for four years."

Candide, curious by nature, let the abbé take him to the lady's house in the Faubourg Saint-Honoré. A faro game was in progress when they arrived. There were twelve gloomy players, each holding a little stack of cards, a dog-eared record of his misfortunes. Deep silence reigned; the players' faces were pale, the banker's was tense. The lady of the house was sitting beside this merciless banker, and her sharp eyes instantly spotted all the players who fraudulently dog-eared their cards[9]. She made them unbend the corners with strict but polite attention, and never showed any anger, for fear of losing her clients. She had given herself the title of Marquise de Parolignac[10]. Her fifteen-year-old daughter sat at the table with the others and warned her mother with a wink each time one of the poor players tried to repair the ravages of fortune by cheating. When the abbé, Candide and Martin walked in, no one stood up, greeted them or even looked at them; everyone was profoundly occupied with the cards. "Baroness Thunder-ten-tronckh was more civil," said Candide.

Meanwhile the abbé was saying something in the marquise's ear. She stood up halfway, honored Candide with a gracious smile and gave Martin a thoroughly dignified nod. She offered Candide a seat and a seat of cards. He lost fifty thousand francs in two draws, after which they all sat down to supper in good spirits. Everyone was surprised by Candide's lack of concern over his loss. The footmen said to each other, in their footman language, "He must be some English milord."

The supper was like most Parisian suppers: silence at first, then a burst of unintelligible chatter, then witticisms that were mostly vapid, false rumors, bad reasonings, a little politics and a great deal of slander; they even spoke about new books.

"Have you seen," said the abbé, "the new novel written by Monsieur Gauchat, Doctor of Theology?"

"Yes," replied one of the guests, "but I couldn't finish it. All kinds of senseless things have been written, but the writings of Monsieur Gauchat, Doctor of Theology, are the most senseless of all. I'm so disgusted with the enormous mass of abominable books with which we're flooded that I've taken to playing faro."

"And what about Archdeacon T——'s[11] essays?" said the abbé. "What do you think of them?"

"Oh, what a deadly bore!" said the Marquise de Parolignac. "What pains he takes to tell you things everyone already knows! How heavily he discusses things that aren't even worth being passed over lightly! How witlessly he takes over other people's wit! How he spoils everything he steals! How he disgusts me! But he won't disgust me any more: I've read a few of the archdeacon's pages, and that's enough."

Seated at the table was a man of learning and good taste who confirmed what the marquise had said. The conversation then turned to tragedies. The marquise asked why there were tragedies which were sometimes performed, but which were unreadable. The man of good taste explained quite clearly how a play could arouse some interest, yet have no merit. He proved in a few words that it is not enough to bring in one or two of those situations which are found in novels and which always captivate an audience; but that a dramatist must be original without being eccentric, that he must be often sublime and always natural, that he must know the human heart and make it speak, be a great poet without letting any of his characters sound like a poet, have a perfect command of his language and write it with purity and continuous harmony, without ever sacrificing meaning to rhyme. "A playwright who doesn't observe these rules," he added, "may turn out one or two tragedies that will be applauded in the theater, but he'll never be regarded as a good writer. There are very few good tragedies. Some tragedies are actually idyls in well-written and well-rhymed dialogue; some are political arguments that put you to sleep, or long-winded dissertations that exasperate you; others are wild ravings written in a barbarous style, filled with disconnected chatter, long declamations to the gods because the author doesn't know how to speak to men, false maxims, and bombastic commonplaces."

Candide listened attentively to these remarks and

conceived a high opinion of the speaker. Since the marquise had been careful to seat him beside her, he leaned close to her ear and took the liberty of asking her who that man was who spoke so well.

"He's a scholar," said the marquise, "who never plays faro. The abbé occasionally brings him to my house for supper. He knows all about tragedies and books; he's written a tragedy that was hissed when it was performed, and a book that has never been seen outside his bookseller's shop, except for one inscribed copy which he sent to me."

"What a great man!" said Candide. "He's another Pangloss!" Then, turning toward him, he said, "Sir, am I right in assuming that you think everything is for the best in the physical and moral world, and that things could not have been otherwise?"

"Sir, I think nothing of the sort," replied the scholar. "It seems to me that everything is going wrong in this country, that no one knows his rank or his responsibilities, and that except during supper, when people are in rather good spirits and seem to get along with each other fairly well, the rest of the time is spent in senseless quarrels: Jansenists against Molinists, Parliament against Church, men of letters against men of letters, courtiers against courtiers, financiers against the people, wives against husbands, relatives against relatives; it's an endless war."

"I've seen worse," replied Candide. "But a wise man, who later had the misfortune to be hanged, taught me that such things are exactly as they should be: they're the shadows in a beautiful picture."

"Your hanged philosopher was an arrogant jester," said Martin. "Your shadows are actually horrible blemishes."

"The blemishes are made by men," said Candide. "They can't avoid making them."

"Then it's not their fault," said Martin.

Most of the gamblers, to whom this talk was unintelligible, were drinking. Martin began a discussion with the scholar while Candide recounted part of his adventures to the lady of the house.

After supper, the marquise took Candide into her boudoir and invited him to sit down on a couch.

"So you're still madly in love with Lady Cunegonde of Thunder-ten-tronckh?" she said to him.

"Yes, madam," replied Candide.

"You answer me like a young man from Westphalia," said the marquise with a tender smile. "A Frenchman would have said to me, 'It's true that I once loved Lady Cunegonde, but now that I've seen you, Madam, I'm afraid I'm no longer in love with her.'"

"I'm sorry, madam," said Candide. "I'll answer you any way you like."

"Your passion for her," said the marquise, "began when you picked up her handkerchief; I want you to pick up my garter."

"I'll be glad to," said Candide, and he picked it up.

"And now I want you to put it on me," said the lady, and Candide put it on her.

"You see," she said, "you're a foreigner; I sometimes make my Parisian lovers languish for two weeks, but I'm giving myself to you the first night, because a lady ought to do the honors of her country to a young man from Westphalia."

Having noticed two enormous diamonds on the young foreigner's hand, she praised them so enthusiastically that they passed from his fingers to hers.

After leaving the marquise's house with the abbé, Candide felt some remorse over having been unfaithful to Lady Cunegonde, and the abbé shared his sorrow. He had received only a small part of the fifty thousand francs Candide had lost at cards, and of the value of the two diamonds that had been half extorted from him. His plan was to draw as much profit as he could from any advantages his acquaintance with Candide might bring him. He talked to him a great deal about Cunegonde, and Candide told him he would beg her to forgive him when he saw her again in Venice.

The abbé redoubled his amiable attentions. He took

an affectionate interest in everything Candide said, everything he did, everything he wanted to do.

"So you're going to meet her in Venice?" he said.

"Yes," replied Candide, "I absolutely must go and find Lady Cunegonde." Then, carried along by the pleasure of speaking about the object of his love, he related, as he was wont to do, part of his adventures with that illustrious Westphalian lady.

"Lady Cunegonde must be highly intelligent," said the abbé, "and she must write charming letters."

"I've never had a letter from her," said Candide. "After being driven from the castle because of my love for her, I naturally couldn't write to her, then shortly afterward I learned that she was dead, then I found her again, then I lost her, and now I've sent a messenger to her, six thousand miles from here, and I'm waiting for an answer."

The abbé listened attentively and seemed thoughtful. He soon took leave of the two foreigners, after giving them each an affectionate embrace. When Candide awoke the next morning he received a letter worded as follows:

My dearest love,
I have been ill in this city for a week now, and I have just learned that you are also here. I would fly to your arms if I could move. I was told about your voyage to Bordeaux; I left the faithful Cacambo and the old woman there, and I expect them to join me here soon. The Governor of Buenos Aires took everything, but I still have your heart. Come to me; your presence will either bring me back to life or make me die of pleasure.

This charming and unexpected letter filled Candide with inexpressible joy, and the illness of his dear Cunegonde overwhelmed him with sorrow. Torn between these two sentiments, he took his gold and diamonds and went with Martin to the hotel where Lady Cunegonde was staying. He walked in trembling with emotion, his heart pounding, his voice choked by sobs. He tried to draw back the bed curtains and wanted to have some light brought in, but the maid said to him, "No, you mustn't: light would kill her," and abruptly closed the curtains again.

"My dearest Cunegonde," said Candide, weeping, "how do you feel? If you can't see me, at least speak to me."

"She can't speak," said the maid.

The lady then put out a plump hand from the bed; Candide bathed it with his tears for a long time, then filled it with diamonds, leaving a bag full of gold on the armchair.

In the midst of his rapture an officer of the watch came into the room, followed by the abbé and a squad of soldiers.

"Are these the two suspicious strangers?" he said. He immediately had them seized and ordered his men to take them to prison.

"This isn't the way travelers are treated in Eldorado," said Candide.

"I'm more of a Manichean than ever," said Martin.

"But where are you taking us, sir?" asked Candide.

"To a dungeon," replied the officer.

When he had regained his self-possession, Martin decided that the lady pretending to be Cunegonde was an impostor, that the abbé was a scoundrel who had taken advantage of Candide's innocence as quickly as he could, and that the officer was another scoundrel who could easily be gotten rid of.

Not wishing to expose himself to judicial proceedings, enlightened by Martin's advice and still impatient to see the real Cunegonde, Candide gave the officer three little diamonds worth about thirty thousand francs each.

"Ah, sir," said the man with the ivory stick, "if you'd committed every crime imaginable, you'd still be the most honest man in the world! Three diamonds! Each one worth thirty thousand francs! Sir, I'd rather die than take you to prison. All strangers are being arrested, but leave everything to me; I have a brother at Dieppe, in Normandy—I'll take you there, and if you have a diamond to give him, he'll take care of you the same as I would."

"But why are all strangers being arrested?" asked Candide.

The abbé answered him: "Because a beggar from Artois[12] heard some people talking nonsense, and that was enough to make him try to commit a parricide, not like the one of 1610, in May, but like the one of 1594, in December, and like several others that have been committed in other years and other months by other beggars who had heard people talking nonsense."

The officer then explained what the abbé was referring to.

"Oh, the monsters!" cried Candide. "What! Can such horrors occur among a people who sing and dance? I'm eager to get out of this country where monkeys harass tigers. I've seen bears in my country, but I've seen men only in Eldorado. In the name of God, sir, take me to Venice, where I must wait for Lady Cunegonde."

"I can take you only to Lower Normandy," said the officer.

He immediately had the irons removed, said he had been mistaken, sent his men away and took Candide and Martin to Dieppe, where he left them in the hands of his brother. There was a small Dutch ship in the harbor. The Norman, who, with the help of three diamonds, had been made into the most obliging of men, embarked Candide and his retinue on this ship, which was about to sail for Portsmouth, in England. It was not the way to Venice, but Candide felt that he had just been delivered from hell and expected to resume his journey to Venice at the first opportunity.

CHAPTER XXIII

*How Candide and Martin reached the coast of
England, and what they saw there.*

Oh, Pangloss! Pangloss! Oh, Martin! Martin! Oh, my
dear Cunegonde! What kind of a world is this?" said
Candide on the Dutch ship.

"It's something insane and abominable," replied
Martin.

"You know England: are people as mad there as in
France?"

"It's another kind of madness," said Martin. "As you
know, those two nations are fighting a war over a few
acres of snow on the edge of Canada, and they're
spending more on that glorious war than the whole of
Canada is worth. It's beyond my feeble powers to tell
you whether there are more raving lunatics in one
country than in another. All I know is that the people
we're about to see are extremely moody and morose."

Talking thus, they arrived at Portsmouth. The shore
was covered with a large crowd of people. They were
all looking attentively at a rather stout man who was
kneeling, blindfolded, on the deck of a naval vessel.
There were four soldiers standing opposite him; they
each calmly fired three bullets into his head, and the
crowd walked away with great satisfaction.

"What was all that?" said Candide. "And what
demon exercises his power everywhere?" He asked
who the stout man was who had just been ceremoni-
ously killed.

"An admiral[13]," was the reply.

"And why was that admiral killed?"

"Because he didn't kill enough men. He fought a
battle with a French admiral, and it was decided that
he wasn't close enough to him."

"But," said Candide, "the French admiral was just
as far away from the English admiral."

"That's undeniable," was the answer. "But in this country it's good to kill an admiral now and then, to encourage the others."

Candide was so bewildered and shocked by what he had seen and heard that he would not even set foot on shore: he made a bargain with the Dutch captain (even at the risk of being robbed by him as he had been robbed by the captain from Surinam) to take him to Venice without delay.

The captain was ready two days later. They sailed along the coast of France. They passed within sight of Lisbon, and Candide shuddered. They sailed through the straits and into the Mediterranean. Finally they landed at Venice.

"God be praised!" said Candide, embracing Martin. "This is where I'll see the fair Cunegonde again. I trust Cacambo as I would myself. All is well, everything is going well, things are going as well as they possibly can."

CHAPTER XXIV

Paquette and Brother Giroflée.

As soon as he was in Venice, he looked for Cacambo in all the inns and cafés, and asked all the women of easy virtue about him, but he did not find him. Every day he sent messengers to all incoming ships and boats. No news of Cacambo.

"How can this be?" he said to Martin. "I've had time to go from Surinam to Bordeaux, from Bordeaux to Paris, from Paris to Dieppe, and from Dieppe to Portsmouth, then sail down the coast of Spain and Portugal, cross the Mediterranean and spend several months in Venice, and still the fair Cunegonde hasn't come! Instead of her, I've met only an infamous wench and an abbé from Périgord! Cunegonde must be dead, and the only thing left for me is to die too. Oh, it would have been better to stay in the paradise of Eldorado, instead of coming back to this devilish Europe. How right you are, my dear Martin! Life is nothing but illusions and calamities!"

He sank into black melancholy and would have nothing to do with the *opera alla moda* or the other amusements of the carnival; not one lady made him feel the slightest temptation.

"You certainly are naïve," said Martin, "to imagine that a half-breed valet, with five or six million in his pocket, will go to find your mistress at the end of the world and bring her to you here in Venice. If he finds her, he'll take her for himself; if he doesn't he'll take another woman. I advise you to forget about your valet Cacambo and your mistress Cunegonde."

Martin was not very comforting. Candide's melancholy increased, and Martin was constantly proving to him that there was little virtue or happiness in the world, except perhaps in Eldorado, where no one could go.

One day as he was discussing this important question and waiting for Cunegonde, Candide saw a young Theatine monk in St. Mark's Square, arm in arm with a girl. The monk appeared to be healthy, plump and vigorous; he had bright eyes, an air of self-assurance, a firm countenance and a proud bearing. The girl was very pretty; she sang as she walked with her monk, gazed at him amorously and pinched his chubby cheeks from time to time.

"You'll at least admit that those two are happy," said Candide to Martin. "Till now I've met nothing but unfortunate people in all the inhabitable world, except in Eldorado, but I'll bet that girl and that monk are very happy."

"I'll bet they're not," said Martin.

"All we have to do is to invite them to dinner," said Candide, "and you'll see if I'm wrong."

He immediately went up to them, paid his respects to them and invited them to his inn to eat macaroni, Lombardy partridges and caviar, with Lachryma Christi and wines from Montepulciano, Cyprus and Samos. The young lady blushed; the monk accepted

the offer and she followed him, looking at Candide in surprise and embarrassment, her eyes dimmed by a few tears. As soon as she entered his bedroom she said to him, "What! Don't you recognize Paquette, Master Candide?"

At these words Candide, who had not looked at her attentively till then, because he was still preoccupied with Cunegonde, said to her, "Alas, poor child, so you're the one who put Dr. Pangloss in such fine condition!"

"Alas, sir, it's true," said Paquette. "I see you know all about it. I've heard of the terrible things that happened to the baroness's whole household, including the fair Cunegonde. And I swear my fate has been just as sad. I was completely innocent when you first saw me. A Franciscan friar who was my confessor easily seduced me, and the results were horrible. I was forced to leave the castle a short time after the baron had driven you away with hard kicks in the behind. If a famous doctor hadn't taken pity on me, I'd have died. I became his mistress for a while, out of gratitude. His wife was violently jealous, and she beat me unmercifully every day; she was a Fury. The doctor was the ugliest man in the world, and I was the most miserable creature alive, from being constantly beaten for a man I didn't love. You know, sir, how dangerous it is for a shrewish woman to be a doctor's wife. One day, exasperated by her behavior, he gave her some medicine for a slight cold, and it worked so well that she died two hours later in horrible convulsions. Her family tried to have him arrested for murder, but he ran away and I was put in prison. My innocence would have saved me if I hadn't been rather pretty. The judge released me on condition that I let him take the doctor's place. I was soon supplanted by a rival, driven away without any compensation and forced to continue that abominable trade which seems so pleasant to you men, but which is nothing but an abyss of misery for us. I came to Venice to practice my profession. Oh, sir, if you could only imagine what it's like to be forced to caress without discrimination an old merchant, a lawyer, a monk, a gondolier or a priest, to be exposed to every kind of insult and abuse, to be often reduced to borrowing a skirt for some disgusting man to lift up, to be robbed by one man of what you've earned with another, to be blackmailed by magistrates, and to have nothing to look forward to except an atrocious old age, the workhouse and the garbage dump, you'd conclude that I'm one of the most wretched creatures in the world!"

It was thus that Paquette opened her heart to the kindly Candide as they sat in a small private room with Martin.

"You see: I've already won half the bet," said Martin to Candide.

Brother Giroflée had remained in the dining room and was having a drink while he waited for dinner.

"But you looked so gay and happy when I met you!" Candide said to Paquette. "You were singing and caressing your monk with such natural affection! You seemed as happy then as you now claim to be unfortunate."

"Oh, sir," replied Paquette, "that's one more misery of my profession. Yesterday I was robbed and beaten by an officer, and today I must appear to be in a cheerful mood to please a monk."

Candide had heard enough: he admitted that Martin was right. They sat down to table with Paquette and the monk. The meal was rather enjoyable, and by the end of it they were talking to one another with a certain intimacy.

"Father," Candide said to the monk, "you seem to be leading a life that anyone would envy: you're obviously in the pink of health, your face is aglow with happiness, you have a pretty girl for your recreation, and you appear to be quite content with your lot as a Theatine monk."

"Believe me, sir," said Brother Giroflée, "I wish the Theatines were all at the bottom of the sea. I've been tempted a hundred times to set fire to the monastery and go off and become a Turk. My parents forced me to put on this hateful robe at the age of fifteen, so that they could leave a larger fortune to my cursed elder brother, may the devil take him! The monastery is filled with jealousy, discord and anger. It's true that I've preached a few bad sermons that have brought me a little money—the prior steals half of it and I spend the rest on women—but each time I go back to the monastery at night I'm ready to smash my head against the wall of the dormitory, and all the other monks feel the same."

Martin turned to Candide with his usual composure and said, "Well, haven't I won the whole bet?"

Candide gave Paquette two thousand piasters and Brother Giroflée a thousand.

"I assure you they'll be happy with that," he said.

"I'm sure they won't," said Martin. "It may be that those piasters will make them unhappier than before."

"Perhaps so," said Candide, "but one thing consoles me: I've learned that we often come across people we thought we'd never see again. Since I've found my red sheep and Paquette, it's quite possible that I'll also find Cunegonde."

"I hope she'll make you happy some day," said Martin, "but I strongly doubt it."

"You're a bitter man," said Candide.

"That's because I've lived," said Martin.

"But look at those gondoliers: they're always singing," said Candide.

"You don't see them at home, with their wives and their little brats," said Martin. "The doge has his troubles, and gondoliers have theirs. It's true that, on the whole, a gondolier's life is preferable to a doge's, but I think the difference is so small that it's not worth examining."

"I've been told about a senator named Pococurante[14]," said Candide, "who lives in a beautiful palace on the Brenta and always gives strangers a courteous welcome. They say he's a man who's never known sorrow or trouble."

"I'd like to see such a rare specimen," said Martin.

Candide immediately sent Signor Pococurante a request for permission to visit him the following day.

CHAPTER XXV

A visit to Signor Pococurante,
Venetian nobleman.

CANDIDE and Martin got into a gondola which took them down the Brenta to the palace of the noble Pococurante. The gardens were well laid out and adorned with beautiful marble statues, and the palace was an architectural triumph. The master of the house, a wealthy man in his early sixties, received his two visitors with great courtesy but very little enthusiasm, which disconcerted Candide and did not displease Martin.

Two pretty, well-dressed girls served them with cups of frothy chocolate. Candide could not help praising their beauty, graciousness and dexterity.

"They're rather pleasant girls," said Senator Pococurante. "I sometimes take them to bed with me, because I'm tired of the ladies of the city, with their coquettishness, jealousy, quarrels, moods, pettiness, pride and foolishness, as well as the sonnets you have to write or have written for them. But those two girls are beginning to bore me too."

Later, as they were strolling down a long gallery, Candide was surprised by the beauty of the pictures he saw. He asked which master had painted the first two.

"They're by Raphael," said the senator. "I paid a high price for them several years ago, out of vanity. They're said to be two of the finest paintings in Italy, but I don't like them at all: the colors are too dark, the figures aren't well shaded and don't stand out enough, and the draperies don't look at all like cloth. In short, no matter what anyone may say, I find no true imitation of nature in them. I'll like a painting only if it makes me think I'm seeing nature itself, but there are no such paintings. I have many pictures, but I no longer look at them."

Pococurante had a concerto performed before dinner. Candide found the music delightful.

"That noise may be amusing for half an hour," said Pococurante, "but if it lasts any longer it bores everyone, although no one dares to admit it. Music nowadays is nothing but the art of composing and performing difficult pieces, and things that are merely difficult never give lasting pleasure.

"I might like opera more if they hadn't managed to make it into a monstrosity that revolts me. Anyone who wants to can go to see bad tragedies set to music, in which the scenes are written only to give flimsy pretexts for two or three wretched songs that show off some actress's windpipe; I have nothing against those who are willing or able to swoon with pleasure when they see a eunuch warbling the part of Caesar or Cato and moving awkwardly around the stage; but for my part, I've long since given up such pitiful nonsense, which is now the glory of Italy, and for which sovereigns pay such large sums."

Candide argued a little, but with discretion. Martin agreed with the senator wholeheartedly.

They sat down to table; then, after an excellent dinner, they went into the library. Candide saw a magnificently bound Homer and complimented the illustrious nobleman on his good taste. "Here's a book," he said, "that used to delight the great Pangloss, the best philosopher in Germany."

"It doesn't delight me," said Pococurante coldly. "I was once made to believe that I enjoyed reading it, but that constant repetition of combats that are all alike, those gods who are always active but never do anything decisive, that Helen who's the cause of the war but almost never appears in the story, that Troy which is forever besieged but never taken—all those things bored me to tears. I've sometimes asked learned men if they found the book as boring as I do. Those who were sincere all admitted that it put them to sleep whenever they tried to read it, but said that a man must always have it in his library as a relic of antiquity, like those rusty coins that can't be placed in circulation."

"Your Excellency must have a different opinion of Virgil," said Candide.

"I admit," said Pococurante, "that the second, fourth and sixth books of his *Aeneid* are excellent; but as for his pious Aeneas, his stalwart Cloanthes, his faithful Achates, his little Ascanius, his idiotic King Latinus, his vulgar Amata and his insipid Lavinia, I can't think of anything colder or more unpleasant. I prefer Tasso, and Ariosto's cock-and-bull stories."

"May I take the liberty of asking you, sir," said Candide, "if you take pleasure in reading Horace?"

"He wrote a number of maxims which a man of the world can put to good use," said Pococurante, "and the fact that they're expressed in lively verse makes them easier to remember. But I care very little for his journey to Brindusium, or his description of a bad dinner, or his uncouth quarrel between a man named something like Pupilus, whose words, he says, 'were full of pus,' and another man whose words 'were vinegar.' I read with extreme distaste his coarse verses against old women and witches, and I don't see what merit there can be in telling his friend Maecenas that if he places him in the ranks of lyric poets he'll strike his sublime forehead against the stars. Fools admire everything in a celebrated author. I read only for myself, and I like only what suits me personally."

Candide, who had been brought up never to judge anything for himself, was astonished by what he was hearing. Martin found Pococurante's way of thinking quite sensible.

"Oh, here's a Cicero!" said Candide. "Surely you never tire of reading that great man!"

"I never read him," replied the Venetian. "What does it matter to me that he pleaded for Rabirius and Cluentius? I have enough cases of my own to judge. His philosophical works would have suited me better, but when I saw that he doubted everything, I concluded that I knew as much as he did, and that I didn't need anyone's help to be ignorant."

"Ah, here are eighty volumes of the proceedings of a scientific academy!" exclaimed Martin. "There may be something good in them."

"There would be," said Pococurante, "if only one of the authors of that hodgepodge had invented even the art of making pins; but in all those books there are nothing but vain systems and not one useful thing."

"Look at all those plays!" said Candide. "In Italian, Spanish, French . . ."

"Yes," said the senator, "there are three thousand of them, and not three dozen good ones. As for those collections of sonnets, which all together are not worth one page of Seneca, and all those fat volumes of theology, I'm sure you can understand why they're never opened, by me or anyone else."

Martin saw some shelves filled with English books. "I think," he said, "that any republican would enjoy reading most of those works written with so much freedom."

"Yes," replied Pococurante, "it's a fine thing to write what you believe; it's the privilege of man. In Italy we write only things we don't really believe: those who live in the country of the Caesars and the Antonines don't dare to have an idea without the permission of a Dominican. I'd have a high regard for the freedom that inspires the English thinkers if everything admirable in that precious freedom weren't corrupted by passion and party spirit."

Candide noticed a Milton and asked the senator if he regarded that author as a great man.

"Who?" said Pococurante. "That barbarian who makes a long commentary on the first chapter of Genesis in ten books of rough verse? That crude imitator of the Greeks, who disfigures the Creation, and who, instead of representing the Eternal Being creating the universe with His words, makes the Messiah take a big compass from the cupboard of heaven to draw up a plan of His work? Do you expect me to admire a man who spoils Tasso's hell and devil, who disguises Lucifer sometimes as a toad and sometimes as a Pygmy, who make him say the same things over and over again, who makes him argue about theology, who seriously imitates Ariosto's comic invention of firearms and makes the devils fire cannons in heaven? Neither I nor anyone else in Italy could enjoy those pitiful absurdities. The marriage of Sin and Death, and the snakes which Sin gives birth to, are enough to sicken a man with any delicacy of taste. And his long description of a hospital would please only a gravedigger. That obscure, grotesque and disgusting poem was despised at its birth; I now treat it as it was treated in its own country by its author's contemporaries. Furthermore, I always say what I think, and I don't care whether others agree with me or not."

Candide was distressed by these statements. He respected Homer and had some liking for Milton. "Alas," he whispered to Martin, "I'm afraid this man may have utter contempt for our German poets."

"There wouldn't be much harm in that," said Martin.

"Oh, what a superior man!" said Candide under his breath. "What a great genius this Pococurante is! Nothing can please him."

When they had thus gone over all of Pococurante's books, they went downstairs to the garden. Candide praised all its beauties.

"I know of nothing in such bad taste," said the master of the house. "There's nothing here but worthless trifles; but tomorrow I'm going to have work begun on a more nobly designed garden."

When the two visitors had taken leave of His Excellency, Candide said to Martin, "Well, you'll have to admit that there's the happiest man alive, because he's above everything he owns."

"Can't you see," said Martin, "that he's disgusted with everything he owns? As Plato said long ago, the best stomachs are not those which reject all foods."

"But," said Candide, "isn't there pleasure in criticizing everything? In being aware of defects where other men see beauties?"

"Do you mean," said Martin, "that there's pleasure in having no pleasure?"

"I suppose not," said Candide. "In that case, I'll be the only happy man in the world, when I see Lady Cunegonde again!"

"It's always good to hope," said Martin.

Days and weeks went by, however, and Cacambo did not come. Candide was so deeply immersed in his sorrow that it did not occur to him that Paquette and Brother Giroflée had never even returned to thank him.

CHAPTER XXVI

How Candide and Martin had supper with six foreigners, and who they were.

ONE evening as Candide and Martin were about to sit down to table with the other foreigners who were staying at their inn, a man with a soot-colored face came up behind Candide, took him by the arm and said, "Be ready to leave with us, without fail."

Candide turned around and saw Cacambo. Only the sight of Cunegonde could have surprised and delighted him more. He was nearly mad with joy. He embraced his dear friend and said, "Cunegonde must be here too: where is she? Take me to her, let me die of joy with her."

"Cunegonde isn't here," said Cacambo, "she's in Constantinople."

"Good heavens! Constantinople! But I'd fly to her even if she were in China! Let's go!"

"We'll leave after supper," said Cacambo. "I can't tell you any more than that. I'm a slave. My master is waiting for me: I have to go and serve him at table. Don't say a word. Eat your supper and be ready."

Candide was torn between joy and sorrow; he was

delighted to see his faithful friend again, and astonished to see him a slave; he was filled with the idea of
finding his mistress again, his heart was agitated, and
his mind was in a turmoil. He sat down to table with
Martin, who regarded all those adventures with detachment, and with six foreigners who had come to Venice
for the carnival.

Cacambo, who had been pouring wine for one of
the six foreigners, leaned close to his master's ear toward the end of the meal and said to him, "Sire, Your
Majesty may leave when he wishes: the ship is ready."
Having said these words, he left the room. The others
sitting around the table were looking at each other in
astonished silence when another servant came up to
his master and said to him, "Sire, Your Majesty's carriage is at Padua, and the boat is ready." The master
made a sign and the servant left. The others looked
at each other again, and the common surprise redoubled. A third valet came up to a third foreigner
and said to him, "Sire, believe me, Your Majesty
mustn't stay here any longer; I'll make all the preparations."

Candide and Martin were by now convinced that
they were witnessing a masquerade that was part of
the carnival. A fourth servant said to a fourth master,
"Your Majesty may leave when he wishes," and went
out as the others had done. A fifth valet said the same
thing to a fifth master. But the sixth valet spoke
differently to the sixth foreigner, who was sitting
near Candide: "Sire," he said, "they won't give any
more credit to Your Majesty, or to me either, and we
may both be in jail before the night is over. I'm going
to take care of my own affairs. Good-by."

When all the servants had disappeared, Candide,
Martin and the six foreigners sat in deep silence. It
was Candide who finally broke it. "Gentlemen," he
said, "this is an odd joke. Why are you all kings? For
my part, I confess that neither Martin nor I are kings."

Cacambo's master replied gravely in Italian: "I'm
not joking. My name is Ahmed III. I was a great sultan
for many years. I dethroned my brother, and my

nephew dethroned me. My viziers were beheaded. I'm now finishing out my life in the old seraglio. My nephew, Sultan Mahmud, sometimes allows me to travel for my health, and I've come to Venice for the carnival."

A young man sitting beside Ahmed spoke next: "My name is Ivan," he said. "I was once Emperor of all the Russias, but I was dethroned while I was still in the cradle. My parents were placed in confinement and I was brought up in prison. I'm sometimes given permission to travel, accompanied by my guards, and I've come to Venice for the carnival."

The third said: "I'm Charles Edward, King of England. My father ceded me his rights to the throne, and I fought to maintain them. The hearts of eight hundred of my followers were torn out and thrown in their faces. I was put in prison. I'm on my way to visit my father, a dethroned king like my grandfather and myself, and I've come to Venice for the carnival."

The fourth then spoke: "I'm the King of Poland; the fortunes of war deprived me of my hereditary dominions, and my father suffered the same fate. I've placed myself in the hands of Providence, like Sultan Ahmed, Emperor Ivan and King Charles Edward, to whom God grant long life, and I've come to Venice for the carnival."

The fifth said: "I'm also King of Poland; I lost my kingdom twice, but Providence gave me another realm, in which I've done more good than all the kings of the Sarmatians put together were ever able to do on the banks of the Vistula. I've also placed myself in the hands of Providence, and I've come to Venice for the carnival."

It was now time for the sixth monarch to speak. "Gentlemen," he said, "my lineage isn't as illustrious as yours, but I was once a king like any other. I'm Theodore: I was elected King of Corsica. I was called 'Your Majesty'; now I'm scarcely called 'Sir.' I had money minted, and now I'm penniless; I had two Secretaries of State, and I now have only one valet. I once sat on a throne, and for a long time I lay on a bed of straw in a London prison. I'm afraid I may be given the same treatment here, even though I've come to Venice, like Your Majesties, for the carnival."

The five other kings listened to this speech with noble compassion. They each gave King Theodore twenty sequins with which to buy clothes, and Candide presented him with a diamond worth two thousand sequins. "Who is this ordinary private individual," said the five kings, "who can afford to give a hundred times as much as any of us, and actually gives it?"

As they were leaving the table, there arrived at the same inn four Serene Highnesses who had also lost their dominions through the fortunes of war, and who had come to Venice for the remainder of the carnival. But Candide paid no attention to these newcomers. His mind was occupied solely with going to Constantinople to find his dear Cunegonde.

CHAPTER XXVII

Candide's voyage to Constantinople.

The faithful Cacambo had already spoken to the Turkish captain who was going to take Sultan Ahmed back to Constantinople and obtained his permission for Candide and Martin to come aboard his ship. They both embarked after prostrating themselves before His miserable Highness. On the way to the ship, Candide said to Martin, "We've just had supper with six kings, and I even gave charity to one of them! There may be many other princes who are still more unfortunate. As for me, I've lost nothing but a hundred sheep, and I'm hurrying to Cunegonde's arms. Once again, my dear Martin, Pangloss was right: everything is for the best."

"I hope so," said Martin.

"But what an unlikely adventure we've just had in Venice!" said Candide. "No one ever saw or heard of

107

six dethroned kings having supper together at an inn."

"That's no more extraordinary than most of the things that have happened to us," said Martin. "It's quite common for kings to be dethroned, and as for the honor we've had of eating supper with them, it's a trifle that doesn't deserve our attention."

As soon as Candide was on board the ship he threw his arms around his former valet, his friend Cacambo. "And what is Cunegonde doing now?" he asked him. "Is she still a prodigy of beauty? Does she still love me? Is she in good health? Have you bought her a palace in Constantinople?"

"My dear master," replied Cacambo, "Cunegonde is now washing dishes on the shore of the Sea of Marmora, for a prince who has very few dishes: she's a slave in the house of a former sovereign named Ragotski who's taken refuge in Turkey and is living on a small allowance given to him by the Grand Turk. But what's even sadder is that she's lost her beauty and become horribly ugly."

"Ah, whether she's beautiful or ugly, I'm an honorable man," said Candide, "and my duty is to love her forever. But how can she have been reduced to such a state, with the five or six million you brought her?"

"First of all," said Cacambo, "I had to give two million to Señor Don Fernando de Ibaraa, y Figueora, y Mascarenes, y Lampurdos, y Suza, Governor of Buenos Aires, for his permission to take Lady Cunegonde away. Then a pirate expertly robbed us of all the rest and took us to Matapan, Melos, Ikaria, Samos, Patras, the Dardanelles, Marmora and Scutari. Cunegonde and the old woman are working in the house of the prince I told you about, and I'm the dethroned sultan's slave."

"What a terrible series of calamities!" said Candide. "But, after all, I still have a few diamonds, so I'll easily deliver Cunegonde. It's a pity she's become so ugly."

He then turned to Martin and said, "Which of us do you think is the most unfortunate: Emperor Ahmed, Emperor Ivan, King Charles Edward, or I?"

"I have no idea," said Martin. "I'd have to be inside your hearts to know."

"Ah," said Candide, "if Pangloss were here he'd know and tell us."

"I don't know what scales your Pangloss would use to weigh the misfortunes of men and judge their sorrows," said Martin. "All I presume is that there are millions of men in this world who are a hundred times more unfortunate than King Charles Edward, Emperor Ivan and Sultan Ahmed."

"That may well be true," said Candide.

A few days later they reached the Bosporus. Candide began by buying Cacambo's freedom at a very high price, then he and his companions boarded a galley without delay and set off for the shore of the Sea of Marmora to find Cunegonde, however ugly she might be.

Among the galley slaves there were two who rowed very badly, and the Levantine captain occasionally gave them a few lashes on their bare shoulders. Candide naturally looked at them more attentively than the others, and went over to them with pity. Certain features of their disfigured faces seemed to bear a slight resemblance to those of Pangloss and that unfortunate Jesuit, that baron, Lady Cunegonde's brother. This idea troubled Candide, and saddened him. He looked at them still more attentively. "Really," he said to Cacambo, "if I hadn't seen Dr. Pangloss hanged, and if I hadn't had the misfortune to kill the baron, I'd think they were these two men rowing in this galley."

On hearing the names of Pangloss and the baron, the two galley slaves uttered a loud cry, sat still on their benches and dropped their oars. The Levantine captain rushed up to them and the lashes rained down more heavily than ever.

"Stop, sir, stop!" cried Candide. "I'll give you as much money as you want."

"What! It's Candide!" said one of the galley slaves.

"What! It's Candide!" said the other.

"Is this a dream?" said Candide. "Am I awake? Am

I really in this galley? Is this the baron I killed? Is this the Dr. Pangloss I saw hanged?"

"Yes, it is, it is!" they replied.

"Tell me, Levantine captain," said Candide, "how much money do you want for the ransom of Lord Thunder-ten-tronckh, one of the most eminent barons of the Empire, and of Dr. Pangloss, the most profound metaphysician in Germany?"

"Dog of a Christian," replied the Levantine captain, "since these two dogs of Christian galley slaves are barons and metaphysicians, which is no doubt a high rank in their country, you'll have to give me fifty thousand sequins for them."

"You'll have it, sir: take me back to Constantinople with the speed of lightning and you'll be paid on the spot. But no—take me to Lady Cunegonde."

After hearing Candide's first offer, however, the Levantine captain had already turned his ship toward the city and was making his slaves row it faster than a bird cleaves the air.

Candide embraced the baron and Pangloss again and again. "How is it that I didn't kill you, my dear baron?" he asked. "And you, my dear Pangloss, how is it that you're still alive after being hanged? And why are you both on a Turkish galley?"

"Is it true that my dear sister is in this country?" asked the baron.

"Yes," replied Cacambo.

"I've found my dear Candide again!" cried Pangloss.

Candide introduced them to Martin and Cacambo. They all embraced each other and began talking simultaneously. The galley was flying: it was already in the harbor. A Jew was summoned and Candide sold him a diamond worth a hundred thousand sequins for fifty thousand; the Jew swore by Abraham that he could not give more. Candide immediately paid the ransom of Pangloss and the baron. Pangloss threw himself at his liberator's feet and bathed them with his tears; the baron thanked him with a nod and promised to pay him back the money at the first opportunity.

"But is it possible that my sister is in Turkey?" he asked.

"Nothing is more possible," replied Cacambo, "since she's now washing dishes for a Prince of Transylvania."

Two other Jews were then summoned; Candide sold more diamonds and they all set out in another galley to deliver Cunegonde.

CHAPTER XXVIII

What happened to Candide, Cunegonde, Pangloss, Martin, etc.

Forgive me once again," Candide said to the baron, "forgive me, Reverend Father, for having run you through with my sword."

"Let's say no more about it," replied the baron. "I was a little too hasty, I admit it. But since you want to know how it happened that you saw me as a galley slave, I'll tell you that after I'd been cured of my wound by the brother apothecary of the college, I was captured and taken away by a detachment of Spaniards. I was imprisoned in Buenos Aires just after my sister had left. I asked to be sent back to Rome to the Father General. I was appointed chaplain to the French ambassador at Constantinople. One evening, less than a week after I'd taken up my duties, I found myself with a very handsome young officer of the sultan's palace. It was hot and the young man decided to bathe, so I took the opportunity to bathe also. I didn't know it was a major crime for a Christian to be found naked with a young Mussulman. A judge had me beaten a hundred times on the soles of the feet and sentenced me to the galleys. I don't think a more horrible injustice has ever been committed. But I'd like to know why my sister is working in the kitchen of a Transylvania sovereign who's taken refuge with the Turks."

"And you, my dear Pangloss," said Candide, "how is it possible that I've found you again?"

"It's true," said Pangloss, "that you saw me hanged, and I was naturally supposed to be burned; but you remember that it began pouring rain when they were about to roast me: the storm was so violent that they gave up hope of lighting the fire. I was hanged because they had nothing better to do. A surgeon bought my body, took me home and began dissecting me. First he made a crucial incision from my navel to my collar-bone. I'd been hanged as badly as anyone could be. The executioner of the Holy Inquisition, a subdeacon, was wonderfully adept at burning people, but he wasn't accustomed to hanging them: the rope was wet and kinked, so it didn't slip properly. In short, I was still breathing. The crucial incision made me let out such a loud yell that my surgeon fell back in terror. Thinking he'd been dissecting the devil, he ran away, dying of fear, and fell down the stairs. Hearing the noise, his wife rushed in from a nearby room and saw me lying on the table with my crucial incision. She was even more frightened than her husband. She ran out of the room and fell on top of him. When they'd both recovered their wits a little, I heard the surgeon's wife say to him, 'Whatever made you decide to dissect a heretic, my dear? Don't you know the devil is always in the bodies of such people? I'll go get a priest to exorcise him right away.'

"I shuddered when I heard this. I gathered the little strength I had left to cry out, 'Have pity on me!' Finally the Portuguese barber regained enough courage to sew up my skin. His wife even took care of me, and two weeks later I was back on my feet. The barber found me a position as servant to a Knight of Malta who was going to Venice, but when I learned that my master didn't have enough money to pay me, I became the servant of a Venetian merchant and went with him to Constantinople.

"One day I took it into my head to enter a mosque.

There was no one inside except an old priest and a pretty young worshiper saying her prayers. She was wearing a dress with a very low neckline, and between her breasts she had a beautiful bouquet of tulips, roses, anemones, buttercups, hyacinths and auriculas. She dropped her bouquet; I picked it up and put it back with zealous respect. I took so long to put it back that the priest became angry, and when he saw I was a Christian he called for help. I was taken before a judge who had me beaten a hundred times on the soles of my feet and sent me to the galleys. I was chained in the very same galley and on the very same bench as the baron. In that galley there were also four young men from Marseilles, five Neapolitan priests and two monks from Corfu. They told us that such things happened every day. The baron claimed that he'd suffered a greater injustice than I had, whereas I maintained that it was much more permissible to return a bouquet to a young woman's chest than to be naked with an officer of the sultan's palace. We were still arguing constantly, and receiving twenty lashes a day, when the chain of events of this universe led you to our galley and you bought our freedom."

"Tell me, my dear Pangloss," said Candide, "when you were hanged, dissected, cruelly beaten and forced to row in a galley, did you still think that everything was for the best in this world?"

"I still hold my original opinions," replied Pangloss, "because, after all, I'm a philosopher, and it wouldn't be proper for me to recant, since Leibniz cannot be wrong, and since pre-established harmony is the most beautiful thing in the world, along with the plenum and subtle matter."

CHAPTER XXIX

How Candide found Cunegonde and the
old woman again.

WHILE Candide, the baron, Pangloss, Martin and Cacambo were relating their adventures, reasoning about the contingent or non-contingent events of this universe, and arguing about cause and effect, moral and physical evil, freedom and necessity, and the consolations that one can find when one is a slave in a Turkish galley, they landed on the shore of the Sea of Marmora, at the house of the Prince of Transylvania. The first thing they saw was Cunegonde and the old woman hanging towels on a line to dry.

The baron turned pale at this sight. When Candide, the tender lover, saw his fair Cunegonde's weather-beaten face, bloodshot eyes, withered breasts, wrinkled cheeks and red, scaly arms, he recoiled three paces in horror, but then he stepped forward out of politeness. She embraced him and her brother; they embraced the old woman; Candide then bought the two women's freedom.

There was a small farm in the vicinity; the old woman suggested that Candide should buy it and that they should all live on it while waiting for their fortunes to take a turn for the better. Cunegonde did not know that she had become ugly, for no one had pointed it out to her. She reminded him of his promises in such a firm tone that the good Candide did not dare to refuse her. He therefore informed the baron that he was going to marry his sister.

"I will never tolerate such baseness on her part, or such insolence on yours," said the baron. "I will never allow myself to be reproached with such a disgrace: my sister's children could not enter the noble assemblies of Germany. No, my sister will never marry anyone but a baron of the Empire."

Cunegonde threw herself at his feet and bathed them with her tears, but he was inflexible.

"You idiot!" cried Candide. "I've rescued you from the galleys and freed you and your sister; she was washing dishes here, and she's ugly, and yet when I'm kind enough to offer to make her my wife, you still claim the right to prevent me! I'd kill you again if I listened to my anger!"

"You can kill me again," said the baron, "but you'll never marry my sister while I'm still alive."

CHAPTER XXX

Conclusion.

At the bottom of his heart, Candide had no desire to marry Cunegonde. But the baron's extreme arrogance determined him to go through with the marriage, and Cunegonde was pressing him so strongly that he could not have taken back his word. He consulted Pangloss, Martin and the faithful Cacambo. Pangloss composed a fine dissertation in which he proved that the baron had no rights over his sister, and that, in accordance with all the laws of the Empire, she and Candide could be joined in a left-handed marriage. Martin advised throwing the baron into the sea. Cacambo decided that he should be returned to the Levantine captain and made a galley slave again, then sent back to the Father General in Rome on the first ship. This was judged to be an excellent idea; the old woman approved of it, and nothing was said to the baron's sister. The plan was carried out with the aid of a little money, and they had the pleasure of triumphing over a Jesuit and punishing the haughtiness of a German baron.

It would be natural to assume that Candide, now married to his mistress after so many disasters, and living with the philosopher Pangloss, the philosopher Martin, the prudent Cacambo and the old woman, and having brought back so many diamonds from the land of the ancient Incas, would lead the most pleasant life in the world. But he had been so cheated by the Jews that he had nothing left but his little farm. His wife, growing uglier every day, became shrewish and unbearable. The old woman was infirm, and even more irascible than Cunegonde. Cacambo, who worked in the garden and went into Constantinople to sell vegetables, was worn out by his work, and cursed his fate. Pangloss was in despair at not being able to shine in some German university. As for Martin, he was finally convinced that people are equally wretched everywhere, so he bore everything with patience. Candide, Martin and Pangloss sometimes discussed metaphysics and morals. From the windows of the house they often saw boats laden with effendis, pashas and cadis who were being exiled to Lemnos, Mytilene or Erzurum. They also saw other cadis, pashas and effendis coming to take the places of the exiles, and then being exiled in their turn. They saw skillfully stuffed heads being taken to the Sublime Porte. These sights stimulated their discussions. But when they were not arguing, their boredom became so oppressive that one day the old woman was driven to say, "I'd like to know which is worse: to be raped a hundred times by Negro pirates, to have one buttock cut off, to run the gauntlet in the Bulgar army, to be whipped and hanged in an auto-da-fé, to be dissected, to be a galley slave—in short, to suffer all the miseries we've all gone through—or to stay here doing nothing."

"That's a hard question," said Candide.

These remarks gave rise to new reflections. Martin concluded that man was born to live in either the convulsions of distress or the lethargy of boredom. Candide did not agree, but he affirmed nothing. Pangloss admitted that he had always suffered horribly, but, having once maintained that all was for the best, he still maintained it, without believing it.

One day something happened which confirmed Martin in his detestable views, made Candide waver more than ever, and disconcerted Pangloss: Paquette and Brother Giroflée arrived at the farm in abject misery. They had quickly squandered their three thousand piasters, parted company with each other, become reconciled, and quarreled again; they had been put in prison, but they had managed to escape, and Brother Giroflée had finally turned Turk. Paquette had continued to ply her trade everywhere, but she no longer earned anything.

"I told you so," said Martin to Candide. "I knew they'd soon spend the money you gave them, and that it would only make them worse off than before. You and Cacambo were once rolling in millions of piasters, and now you're no happier than Brother Giroflée and Paquette."

"Ah, my poor child!" said Pangloss to Paquette. "So heaven has brought you back to us at last! Do you realize that you cost me an eye, an ear and the tip of my nose? Just look at me now! What a world we live in!"

This new turn of events prompted them to philosophize more than ever. There lived in the vicinity a famous dervish who was known as the best philosopher in Turkey; they went to consult him. Acting as their spokesman, Pangloss said to the dervish, "Sir, we've come to ask you why such a strange animal as man was ever created."

"Why are you concerned about that?" said the dervish. "Is it any of your business?"

"But, Reverend Father," said Candide, "there's a terrible amount of evil in the world."

"What does it matter whether there's evil or good?" said the dervish. "When His Highness sends a ship to Egypt, does he worry about whether the mice in it are comfortable?"

"Then what ought we to do?" asked Pangloss.

"Keep quiet," said the dervish.

"I'd been looking forward with pleasure," said Pangloss, "to having a little discussion with you about cause and effect, the best of all possible worlds, the origin of evil, the nature of the soul, and pre-established harmony."

At these words the dervish slammed the door in their faces.

While this conversation was taking place, the news had spread that two viziers and the mufti had been strangled in Constantinople, and that several of their friends had been impaled. This catastrophe caused great commotion for several hours. On their way back to the little farm, Pangloss, Candide and Martin saw a kingly-looking old man sitting in front of his door beneath an arbor of orange trees, enjoying the fresh air. Pangloss, who was as curious as he was argumentative, asked him the name of the mufti who had just been strangled.

"I don't know," replied the old man. "I've never known the name of any mufti or any vizier. I know absolutely nothing about the incident you're referring to. I assume that, in general, those who take part in public affairs sometimes perish miserably, and that they deserve it; but I never pay any attention to what goes on in Constantinople. I content myself with sending the fruits of my garden there to be sold."

Having said these words, he invited the strangers into his house. His two daughters and two sons offered them several kinds of fruit-flavored drinks they had made themselves, as well as boiled cream with pieces of candied citron in it, oranges, lemons, limes, pineapples, pistachio nuts, and mocha coffee unmixed with any of the bad coffee that comes from Batavia and the West Indies. Then the good Mussulman's daughters perfumed his three visitors' beards.

"You must have a vast and magnificent estate," Candide said to the Turk.

"I have only twenty acres of land," replied the Turk, "which my children and I cultivate. Our work keeps us free of three great evils: boredom, vice and poverty."

As they were walking back to the farm, Candide deeply pondered the Turk's remarks. He said to Pangloss and Martin, "That good old man seems to have made himself a much better life than the six kings we had the honor of eating supper with."

"High position is a very dangerous thing," said Pangloss, "as philosophers have always pointed out.

For Eglon, King of the Moabites, was assassinated by Ehud, and Absolom was hung by his hair and stabbed with three spears. King Nadab, son of Jeroboam, was killed by Baasha, King Elah by Zimri, Joram by Jehu, Athaliah by Jehoiada; and King Jehoiakim, King Jehoiachin and King Zedekiah were all made slaves. You know the fate of Croesus, Astyages, Darius, Dionysius of Syracuse, Pyrrhus, Perseus, Hannibal, Jugurtha, Ariovistus, Caesar, Pompey, Nero, Otho, Vitellius, Domitian, Richard II of England, Edward II, Henry VI, Richard III, Mary Stuart, Charles I, the three Henrys of France and Emperor Henry IV. You know—"

"I also know," said Candide, "that we must cultivate our garden."

"You're right," said Pangloss, "because when man was put in the Garden of Eden, he was put there 'to dress it and to keep it,' that is, to work; which proves that man was not born to be idle."

"Let's work without theorizing," said Martin; "it's the only way to make life bearable."

The whole group entered into this commendable plan, and each began to exercise his own talents. The little farm yielded abundant crops. Cunegonde was very ugly, it is true, but she soon became an excellent pastry cook. Paquette embroidered, and the old woman took care of the linen. Everyone made himself useful, even Brother Giroflée: he was a good carpenter, and he even became an honest man.

Pangloss sometimes said to Candide, "All events are interconnected in this best of all possible worlds, for if you hadn't been driven from a beautiful castle with hard kicks in the behind because of your love for Lady Cunegonde, if you hadn't been seized by the Inquisition, if you hadn't wandered over America on foot, if you hadn't thrust your sword through the baron, and if you hadn't lost all your sheep from the land of Eldorado, you wouldn't be here eating candied citrons and pistachio nuts."

"Well said," replied Candide, "but we must cultivate our garden."

Notes

1. These are Prussian recruiting sergeants. The Bulgars here represent the Prussians, and the Avars the French, during the Seven Years' War, which was in progress as Voltaire wrote *Candide*.
2. This chapter was inspired by the great Lisbon earthquake of 1755, which destroyed most of the city.
3. *"Note the author's extreme discretion! So far there has been no pope named Urban X; he is afraid to ascribe a bastard daughter to a known pope. What circumspection! What delicacy of conscience!"*—This note is allegedly by Voltaire himself, although it appeared in no edition of *Candide* prior to 1829.
4. "Oh, what a misfortune to be without testicles!"
5. A Jesuit publication which had occasionally attacked Voltaire.
6. Socinianism was a religious doctrine, condemned by the Inquisition in 1559, which denied a number of orthodox tenets, such as the divinity of Christ, the Trinity and eternal punishment.
7. For a time in Paris, extreme unction was refused to anyone who did not have a document, signed by a non-Jansenist priest, certifying that he was not a Jansenist.

8. Fréron, a journalist with whom Voltaire carried on a bitter feud.
9. Players could dog-ear their cards to indicate that they were going to let their winnings ride on the next draw, but some players would try to cheat by dog-earing their cards without having won on the previous draw.
10. From "paroli," the name given to the practice of letting one's winnings ride on the next draw.
11. Abbé Trublet, another enemy of Voltaire's.
12. Robert-François Damiens, who attempted to assassinate Louis XV in 1757.
13. Admiral John Byng, executed in 1757 after his defeat by La Galissonnière.
14. "Caring little."